A real kic

"Mind some of them other animals," the man said. "They're a bit edgy."

"I'll watch out for them," Clint replied.

Clint gave his big gelding some feed and patted his massive neck. Then he picked up his rifle and started out of the stable, passing close by the other occupied stall. All of a sudden the seemingly worn-out horse in the stall kicked out with both hind legs. Clint almost reacted in time to avoid the flashing hooves. The horse's left hind hoof cleaved the air in front of him, but the right caught him on the side of the leg, just below the knee.

Clint cried out as the leg buckled and he fell to the floor.

DON'T MISS THESE
ALL-ACTION WESTERN SERIES
FROM THE BERKLEY PUBLISHING GROUP

THE GUNSMITH by J. R. Roberts
Clint Adams was a legend among lawmen, outlaws, and ladies.
They called him . . . the Gunsmith.

LONGARM by Tabor Evans
The popular long-running series about U.S. Deputy Marshal
Long—his life, his loves, his fight for justice.

SLOCUM by Jake Logan
Today's longest-running action Western. John Slocum rides a
deadly trail of hot blood and cold steel.

BUSHWHACKERS by B. J. Lanagan
An all-new series by the creators of Longarm! The rousing adventures
of the most brutal gang of cutthroats ever assembled—Quantrill's
Raiders.

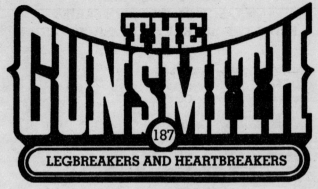

THE GUNSMITH

187

LEGBREAKERS AND HEARTBREAKERS

J. R. ROBERTS

JOVE BOOKS, NEW YORK

LEGBREAKERS AND HEARTBREAKERS

A Jove Book / published by arrangement with
the author

PRINTING HISTORY
Jove edition / July 1997

The Putnam Berkley World Wide Web site address is
http://www.berkley.com

ISBN: 0-515-12105-3

A JOVE BOOK®
Jove Books are published by The Berkley Publishing Group,
200 Madison Avenue, New York, New York 10016.
JOVE and the "J" design are trademarks
belonging to Jove Publications, Inc.

PRINTED IN THE UNITED STATES OF AMERICA

10 9 8 7 6 5 4 3 2 1

THE GUNSMITH 187

LEGBREAKERS AND HEARTBREAKERS

ONE

Of all the places for him to get kicked by a horse, why did it have to be Tucumcari, New Mexico?

Actually, it was his right leg where Clint Adams got kicked, and it was the last thing he expected to have happen. As he rode into Tucumcari his only intention was to make a short rest stop and then continue south until he could cross into West Texas.

Tucumcari had all the charm and appeal of a ghost town, but there were a few people on the street as he entered and looked for the livery stable. When he found it a man who was eighty if he was a day staggered out and stared up at him.

"Kin I help ya?"

"I'd like to put my horse up for a while."

"Welcome ta," the man said. "I'll take him from ya."

Clint made a snap decision not to put Duke, his big black gelding, in the man's care. The man was frail as well as old, and Duke was likely to pull one of his arms out.

"I'll put him up myself, if you don't mind," he said.

"Hell, I don't mind," the man said, taking no insult.

"Less work for me—but ya got to pay the same rate."

"That's no problem," Clint said, dismounting and preparing to walk Duke into the stable.

"Mind some of them other animals," the man said. "They're a bit edgy."

"I'll watch out for them."

As Clint entered the stable he only saw one other stall in use, and the horse there didn't seem all that dangerous. In fact, it looked a bit worn-out.

Clint walked Duke to a stall two down from the other animal and proceeded to unsaddle him and brush him down.

"Don't get too comfortable," he told Duke. "I don't intend to be here all that long."

Clint gave the big gelding some feed and patted his massive neck. Then he picked up his rifle and started out of the stable, passing close by the other occupied stall. All of a sudden the seemingly worn-out horse in that stall kicked out with both hind legs. Clint almost reacted in time to avoid the flashing hooves. The horse's left hind hoof cleaved the air in front of him, but the right caught him on the side of the leg, just below the knee. Clint cried out as the leg buckled and he fell to the floor.

The old man came limping in and asked, "What happened? He kick ya?"

"He sure did," Clint said, reaching for his injured right leg. It hurt like hell, and he thought it might be broken.

"Goddamn it!" he swore, in frustration more than in pain.

"I warned ya, ya can't say I didn't."

"I know you did," Clint said. "You got a doctor in this town?"

''We do.''

Clint moved into a seated position and rubbed his leg. He put his foot down on the ground and tried applying some weight to the leg, but the pain was too bad.

''Want me to fetch 'im?'' the old man asked.

''I guess you better,'' Clint said. ''I don't think I can walk on it.''

''Most likely it's busted.''

''Most likely it is,'' Clint said, shaking his head. It was his own fault. He'd misjudged the horse because of its appearance and had simply walked too close to the stall. The horse wasn't to blame, and neither was the old man.

''I'll get the doc,'' the old man said. ''You wait right there, young fella.''

''I guess I don't have much of a choice,'' Clint said, ''do I?''

The old man chuckled dryly, as if Clint had made a joke, and said, ''No, I guess not.''

TWO

The doctor turned out to be a man almost as old as the liveryman, which explained why it took so long for them to return. By the time they did Clint was sweating from the pain in his leg.

"Just lie still, young man," the doctor said, "and let me have a look."

It seemed to take the man forever to get down on one knee. At one point Clint prepared to catch the man, as he looked as if he was going to fall.

"Can you get your boot off?" the doctor asked.

"I should have thought of that," Clint said. He reached for it and pulled. It was painful, but it came off. Most of the swelling was just above the knee.

"And your trousers? Can you roll the leg up?"

"I don't think so."

"We'll have to take them off, then."

"What, here?"

"There's no one around but us, lad," the doctor said. "Or would you rather I cut the trouser leg?"

"No, no, don't do that," Clint said. "Then I'd have to buy a new pair. I'll try to get them off."

Clint felt odd as the two older men watched him struggle. First he removed his gun belt, and laid it aside, but close at hand. After that he undid his belt and trousers, then lay back and tried to slide them off while bearing his weight on his uninjured leg. It was awkward, but he finally got them down around his ankles.

"All right," the doctor said, "let's have a look at it."

The leg was already turning colors as the doctor probed it. Pain shot from his knee to his ankle, and to his hip.

"It's fractured."

By now Clint could have told the doctor that.

"It doesn't need to be set," the doctor said, "but you'll need to be in a splint and you'll have to stay off of it for a while."

"Damn it!"

The doctor looked up at Clint and smiled. The smile made his weathered face crease up even more.

"Weren't plannin' on stayin' with us too long, were you?"

"No, I wasn't."

"Nobody ever does," the doctor said.

He stood, slowly, and then stared down at Clint.

"I'll need help gettin' you over to my office, and then to the hotel. You'll have to wait here while I fetch a couple of men."

"How long will that take?"

The doctor shrugged.

"It's a small town. Can I get you something in the meanwhile?"

Clint sighed and said, "Some whiskey would help."

"I got a bottle," the liveryman said.

"Get him some, Jake," the doctor said, "and stay with him in case he passes out."

"Right, Doc."

"And get that bottle."

"Right."

"Be right back, Mister . . ."

"Adams," Clint said. "Thanks, Doc."

"Matthews," the doctor said, "Doctor Richard Matthews."

"Thanks, Doctor Matthews."

The doctor nodded, then turned and left the livery. Jake, the liveryman, disappeared and then reappeared with a bottle and a happy look on his face. Clint guessed that this was a good reason for the man to take a drink himself.

"I'll keep you company," the older man said. He took a slug from the bottle, which was half full, then passed it to Clint.

"Thanks."

He took a long drink. It was harsh stuff and it burned all the way down. The burn seemed to meet the pain from his leg halfway, and he took another drink and passed the bottle back to Jake.

"Doc's a good man," Jake said. "He'll fix you up. You'll be good as new in no time."

Clint knew that the only thing that was going to fix him up would be time . . . time that he was going to have to spend in Tucumcari.

He accepted the bottle and took a drink again. They passed it back and forth until it was empty. After that there was nothing to do but wait.

THREE

If Jake the liveryman had had another bottle of whiskey they would have finished that one, too, before the doctor returned with two volunteers to carry Clint to his office. Before they arrived Clint remembered to pull up his trousers and save himself some embarrassment.

"Easy with him, lads," the doctor said as the two men lifted Clint from the ground. "Watch his leg."

The two men carrying Clint were in their thirties, and neither seemed happy about being pulled away from whatever else they were doing.

They carried Clint through the center of town, which didn't attract all that much attention.

"Put him on the table," the doctor said when they reached his small office.

The men deposited Clint on the table, and then the doctor gave them both two dollars and sent them on their way.

"Two dollars apiece?" Clint asked.

"It was the only way I could get them to do it," the doctor said, closing the door behind the two men. He smiled at Clint and added, "Don't worry, I'll add it to your bill. Now let's get that leg fixed up."

7

• • •

The doctor put a wooden splint on Clint's leg, which would immobilize it and keep him from doing any damage to it. He fixed the splint so that there was also a piece of wood running beneath Clint's boot.

"You'll be able to limp over to the hotel on that, but after that I want you to stay off of it."

"For how long?"

"For as long as it takes to heal. You're lucky that horse's kick didn't splinter the bone or break the skin. You'd be looking at four to six weeks if that'd happened."

"And now?"

"I wouldn't count on going anywhere for at least two weeks, maybe more."

"What's there to do in Tucumcari, Doc?" Clint asked.

"Nothin'," the doctor said, "not for the next ten days, anyway."

"And after that?"

"We'll be having our Founder's Day weekend."

"Founder's Day?"

"Sure," Doc Matthews said. "We may be small, but we still have some civic-mindedness."

"I didn't mean any offense, Doc."

"None taken," Matthews said. "See if you can put your weight on that. If you can't I'll have to fetch those lads back and pay them two more dollars apiece to carry you to the hotel."

"I'll walk," Clint said. "I don't want any more money added to my bill."

He slid off the table to the floor, taking his weight on his left leg. Slowly, gingerly, he put his right foot down until he was standing on the splint. It seemed to be taking most of the weight, so that he wasn't hurting the leg.

"It feels okay," he said.

"Walk around the office a bit, let's be sure," Matthews said.

Clint did as he said. It was awkward, but he'd only be walking to the hotel, which was . . .

"Where is the hotel?"

"Two blocks further on," Matthews said. "Can you make it?"

"I'll make it," Clint said, "but I'll need somebody to fetch my saddlebags from the livery."

"I'll have Jake bring them over."

"Will I have to pay him two dollars?" Clint asked good-naturedly.

"The price of a drink should do it, I think."

"I can do that. How much do I owe you, Doc?"

"I don't know yet," Matthews said. "I'll have to figure it out. I'll have a bill brought over to the hotel when I do."

"Fine."

"What's your full name, Mr. Adams?"

"It's Clint Adams, Doc."

Matthews walked to his desk in the corner of the room and wrote Clint's name down.

"Like I said," he repeated, "I'll send a bill over when I've got it all figured out."

"Much obliged, Doc."

Clint left the doctor's office, walking the two blocks to the hotel awkwardly and gingerly. He couldn't tell if the doctor had recognized his name or not. If he had he'd done a hell of a job covering it up. The last thing

Clint needed while he was stuck in Tucumcari for at least two weeks was to attract attention. Still, he hadn't yet taken to registering in hotels under assumed names. Once he signed the register anything could happen.

The doctor had told him to tell the desk clerk that he'd sent him over. Since he was a patient, and stuck in town, Doc Matthews said, there'd be a cheaper room rate for him.

A small favor, Clint thought, and one that would hardly make up for being stuck there.

FOUR

After Clint left Doc Matthews's office the doctor watched until he had limped a block away before leaving his office and hurrying in the other direction. He walked two blocks—practically to the end of town—and went into what was the tallest building in town, the two-story town hall.

"Is he in, Mildred?" he asked as he entered.

"Where else would he be?" Mildred Haskell asked.

Ed Biggers had been mayor of Tucumcari for twenty years, and for all twenty of those Mildred Haskell had been his secretary and—Doc suspected—his lover. Doc's problem with that was that Biggers was perhaps the ugliest man he'd ever seen, and Mildred—even at forty-five or so—was possibly the handsomest woman. It was a match he could never understand, and never prove—and neither could Ed's wife, who was possibly the homeliest woman Doc had ever seen. Indeed, they made an odd trio.

But Ed Biggers ran Tucumcari and he ran it well. It hadn't grown in twenty years, but neither had it gone under like a lot of towns its size.

"I've got to talk to him."

11

"Go on in," Mildred said.

Doc Matthews entered the office without knocking. The only time he didn't do that was when Mildred wasn't at her desk, because he was afraid of what he'd find behind the closed door. He always knocked then, giving them a chance to stop doing whatever it was they were doing—but they never looked like they'd been doing anything.

"Hello, Doc," Biggers said, looking up from his desk. "What's the all-fired hurry?"

"I've got news, Ed," Doc Matthews said, "big news."

Biggers sat back and regarded Doc quizzically.

"Okay, so what is it?"

"Clint Adams is in town."

Biggers sat forward immediately.

"The Gunsmith?"

"That's right."

"What's he doing in town?"

"Just passing through."

"So what's the big news, then?"

"He was over at the livery this morning and Jake's crazy horse kicked him."

"Hurt him bad?"

"Fractured his right leg," Doc said. "He's gonna be in town a few weeks, at least."

"For Founder's Day?" Biggers asked.

Doc grinned.

"He'll be here."

"Hot damn!" Biggers said, sitting back and rubbing his hands together. "We been lookin' for a celebrity for Founder's Day, and one falls right into our laps."

"That's what I was thinkin', as soon as he told me who he was."

"Where is he now?"

"He went over to the hotel."

"Walkin'?"

"I fixed him up so he could walk to the hotel, but that's about as far as he can go."

"You know," Biggers said, "him bein' here could cause trouble. I mean, once the news gets out that the Gunsmith is in Tucumcari . . ."

"I thought about that," Doc said. "Fellas could be comin' here to try him out."

"I wasn't just thinkin' about fellas," the mayor said. "I was thinkin' about the Kid."

Matthews frowned.

"I didn't think of that."

"The Tucumcari Kid isn't one to pass up an opportunity like this one," Biggers pointed out.

"Well, maybe he won't hear about it."

"Oh, he'll hear about it," Biggers said, "but maybe it'll be too late when he does."

"Well," Doc said, "who's gonna ask him?"

Biggers sat back and rubbed his jaw, deep in thought.

"That's somethin' we'll have to decide."

"Well," Matthews said, "he ain't goin' nowhere, but make up your mind quick. It might take some time to convince him."

"Thanks for the information, Doc."

"Sure."

Matthews started for the door and Biggers said, "Hey, Doc?"

"Yeah?"

"Is his leg really fractured," the mayor asked, "or did you just tell him it was?"

"Oh, it's really fractured. Not bad, but it'll keep him here."

"Good," Biggers said, "that's real good."

After Doc left, Mildred came into Biggers's office. She closed the door behind her, just in case.

"What was Doc so excited about?" she asked, sitting across from Biggers.

He told her.

"Do you think you can get him to agree?" she asked.

"He's here, isn't he?" Biggers said. "Why wouldn't he agree?"

"Maybe because he doesn't want to be here," she said. "Maybe while he's here and his leg is healing he'll just want to be left alone."

"Maybe," Biggers said, "and maybe it's just a matter of getting the right person to ask him."

Mildred looked at Biggers suspiciously.

"And just who did you have in mind?"

FIVE

Clint had no trouble getting a room, as the hotel was mostly empty. Also, they had a couple of rooms in the back, on the first floor, so he didn't have to negotiate the stairs.

"Do you have any bags?" the clerk asked. He was a bored-looking man in his forties with dark circles under his eyes. Clint was willing to bet that he had started working there when he was a young man.

Clint wondered if anyone ever came to the Tucumcari Hotel with bags.

"No. Jake will be bringing my saddlebags from the livery, though. Just send him back with them when he comes, huh?"

"Sure."

"And one other thing."

"What's that?"

Clint took out some money and asked, "Could you get me a bottle of whiskey?"

"Good stuff?"

"Not necessarily." Clint knew that if the man bought cheap whiskey there'd be more left over for him. "And keep the change."

"Thanks, mister."

Clint put the money in the man's hand then closed his hand over the other man's.

"But do it quick, huh? I need it for a painkiller."

"I'll get it right away."

"Good."

Once he was in his room he settled down on the bed to wait for his saddlebags, and for his painkiller.

The desk clerk passed Doc Matthews on his way to the saloon.

"What's your hurry, Avery?" Doc asked.

"That new fella you sent over," the clerk answered, "says he wants a bottle of whiskey. He gave me money to buy it."

"If you buy him rotgut and kill him before I can give him my bill, I'll skin you. Understand?"

"B-but he said it didn't have to be the best."

"Just don't get him anything that will kill him. Understand?"

"Sure, Doc. I gotta go."

"Go ahead, then."

Doc continued on to his office. He wondered how long it would take Biggers to decide to send Mildred to talk to Adams about Founder's Day. She was still a handsome woman for her age, and she sure wasn't too old for a man like Clint Adams.

Doc didn't know a man in town who could turn Mildred down when she wanted something.

There was a knock on the door. Clint had decided to leave it unlocked so he wouldn't have to keep getting up and down to answer it. He had his gun belt hanging on his bedpost, easy to get at.

"Come on in."

The door opened and Jake stuck his head in.

"Come on in, Jake."

"I got your saddlebags, like ya asked."

Jake entered, carrying the bags.

"Put them on the bed there at the foot," Clint said, "where I'll be able to reach them."

"Sure thing."

Clint flipped the man a silver dollar, which he deftly caught.

"Much obliged, Mister . . ."

"Adams is the name, Jake," Clint said, "Clint Adams. How's my horse?"

"He's jest fine, Mr. A-adams," Jake stammered. It was obvious he recognized the name.

"Jake, let me ask you something."

"S-sure."

"You get many strangers in town?"

"No, sir, not many."

"Guess people'll be curious about me then, huh?"

"Guess so."

"I'd appreciate it if you didn't talk about me to anyone, Jake. Understand?"

"S-sure, Mr. Adams, I understand."

Clint flipped another dollar through the air and it landed in the palm of Jake's hand.

"If I hear you have been," he said, "I'm going to be real upset."

"Don't you worry, Mr. Adams," Jake said. "Mum's the word with me."

"That's good, Jake," Clint said, "that's real good. Thanks again for the saddlebags."

"Sure thing."

Jake backed out of the room, happy to be away from the man known as the Gunsmith. Sure wasn't safe being around a man like that, silver dollar or no!

It wasn't ten minutes later there was another knock on the door.

"Come ahead."

The door opened and the desk clerk stuck his head in.

"I got your whiskey, Mr. Adams."

"Well, bring it on in . . . what's your name?"

"Avery, sir."

"Bring it in, Avery. Set it down here on the table next to the bed."

Avery came in and put the whiskey down where Clint said, within easy reach. The ache in his leg was bearable for the moment, so he didn't touch it.

As the clerk started for the door, Clint said, "Don't leave yet."

"But I gotta get back—"

"This'll just take a minute," Clint said, and then had roughly the same conversation with Avery that he'd had with Jake. It also cost him the same amount of money.

"You can count on me, Mr. Adams," Avery said finally. "I won't talk to a soul."

"That's fine, Avery. Now, tell me what there is to do in Tucumcari."

"Well, we got church services on Sunday."

"I'm a little more concerned with the rest of the week, Avery."

"Well . . . there's the saloon."

"And what can you do there?"

Avery looked puzzled and said, "Drink."

"And . . . what else?"

"Uh . . ."

"Any gambling?"

"Not really."

"Girls?"

The man actually blushed.

"I don't know. I'm, uh, married. . . ."

"Ah," Clint said. And henpecked, no doubt, since he didn't know much about what went on. "I understand. Thanks."

"Sure."

Avery left and Clint eyed the bottle of whiskey. He decided to wait until the pain got really bad to start hitting it.

He looked at the window, wishing he had opened it before he got on the bed, or asked Avery or Jake to open it before they left. What the hell, he'd just have to close it again when the sun went down.

He leaned back against the pillows, trying to ignore the throbbing in his leg. Finally, he uncorked the bottle and took a sip. Before he knew it, a quarter of the bottle was gone and he was sleepy. He slipped his gun from his holster, held it in his hand, folded his arms across his chest, and in minutes he was asleep.

SIX

Sheriff Caleb York looked up from his desk and smiled as Mildred Haskell entered his office. As usual she was beautiful, her skin smooth and pale, unblemished because she was rarely out in the sun. The scent she was wearing crossed the room and tickled his nose and, as with most of the men in town, the effect traveled down into his pants.

"Mildred," he said, standing, "how nice to see you."

Mildred liked York and, unknown to Ed Biggers or anyone else in town, she had slept with him once or twice. He was about thirty-five, twenty years younger than Biggers, and she found on occasion that she needed a break from the older man. Besides, York was a lot better-looking, though oddly enough, despite his better body, he was not as good in bed as the mayor.

"Sit down, Caleb," Mildred said.

"What brings you here?" the sheriff asked, seating himself. There was hope in his voice. The only two times he had ever slept with Mildred Haskell she had come to him. One day she just walked in, sat down, they shared a cup of coffee and then a drink from the bottle of whiskey he kept in a drawer, and the next thing he knew they were on a cot in one of the cells. It was the most exciting sexual experience Caleb York had ever had, and it had only been repeated once since, and that had been over a year ago.

"The mayor sent me over, Caleb," Mildred said, to dispel any doubt that she might be there for a different reason.

"Oh . . ." York's disappointment was palpable.

"We have a stranger in town, Caleb. Did you know that?"

"Uh, no, I didn't."

"His name's Clint Adams."

The sheriff's disappointment faded and he sat up straight.

"The Gunsmith is in Tucumcari?"

"That's right."

"Why?"

"He was passing through and got kicked in the leg by Jake's crazy horse."

"Is he hurt bad?"

"The leg's fractured," she said. "He'll be here for a while."

"Where is he?"

"At the hotel."

He stood up.

"I should go and talk to him."

"Why?" she asked.

"It's my job."

"Are you going to warn him to stay out of trouble?" she asked. "The man has a fractured leg, Caleb."

"Still—"

"Ed doesn't want him upset," she added.

York frowned.

"Why not?"

"Founder's Day."

He frowned again.

"Think about it."

He didn't, still frowning.

"We need a celebrity," she reminded him.

"Yeah, but the Gunsmith, that might be more trouble than it's worth, Mildred. I mean, if the Kid gets wind of this . . ."

"We'll just have to see that he doesn't," she said, "won't we?"

"How do we do that?"

"You'll have to figure it out," she said. "We'll just have to try to keep it quiet as long as we can."

"Can we do that?"

"It's a small town," she said, and he didn't know if that meant yes or no.

"Then you don't want me to go and talk to Adams?"

She thought a minute.

"I'm going to talk to him," she said, "but maybe you should do it, too, just to be doing your job. You know, just ask him the usual questions."

"The usual questions?"

"You know, what you'd normally ask a stranger."

During the five years he'd been sheriff, Caleb York didn't "normally" deal with strangers, because there were hardly ever any in Tucumcari.

"Uh, okay."

"Why don't you talk to him first," she suggested, "and then I'll go up later."

"Okay."

"I'll tell Ed you're going to do it."

"Fine."

She turned and headed for the door.

"Was that all you wanted, Mildred?" York asked. The hopeful tone was back in his voice.

"Yes, Caleb," she said with a kind smile, "that was all I wanted . . . today."

SEVEN

When the third knock came on the door it was two hours after the first two. Clint had napped for about an hour before the pain woke him. It wasn't actually bad, but it was insistent. He took a couple of drinks and then put the bottle down. Why did a fractured leg seem to hurt worse than any bullet wound he'd ever had?

"Come in," he called out, holding his gun down by his side.

He saw the badge on the man's shirt as he entered, but he still kept his grip on his gun. There was no guarantee that the man was friendly just because he was the law. In fact, it was more than likely that the man wasn't friendly. Clint wasn't always welcome in a lot of towns.

"Mr. Adams?"

"That's right, Sheriff. What can I do for you?"

"Nothin'—well, I mean, I, uh, just wanted to ask you a few questions."

"About what?" Clint asked, shifting on the bed to make himself more comfortable.

"Well . . . uh, I'm really sorry about your, uh, leg."

"Thanks."

"What brought you to Tucumcari in the first place?" the lawman asked.

"I was just passing through, Sheriff," Clint said. "I wanted a hot meal and a drink and then I was going to be on my way."

"I see."

"And then I got kicked—really my own stupid fault—and here I am."

"I see. Uh, how long do you think you'll be here?"

"The doctor said at least two weeks, Sheriff," Clint said. "I'm, uh, hoping to stay out of trouble all that time."

"Well, that's good." The sheriff looked at the gun in Clint's hand.

"Oh, this is just a precaution," Clint said and holstered the gun.

"I see."

Clint had a feeling the sheriff really didn't know what to do next. In fact, he thought the man didn't know what to do at all.

"Was there something else, Sheriff?"

"I, uh, well, you just told me what I wanted to know, really," the sheriff said. "I just didn't want any, uh, trouble."

"I'm hardly in any position to handle trouble, Sheriff," Clint said. "If we can just keep it to ourselves that I'm even here . . ."

"Oh, oh, sure," the sheriff said. "That's a great idea."

"Good, I'm glad you agree."

"I do," the sheriff said.

"Great."

The man stood there in the doorway for a few moments, then said, "Well, I guess that's it."

"Thanks for coming by, Sheriff."

"Sure," the sheriff said, "uh, I hope you get better, uh, soon."

"Thanks."

The sheriff left and closed the door behind him. Clint was left with the distinct impression that someone had sent the man to him and he didn't have the faintest idea how to act.

He swung his legs to the floor and prepared to stand before his butt sprouted roots in the mattress. He stood, taking most of his weight on his good leg to start. He only intended to walk around the room and maybe over to the window. He put his right foot down, pressed a bit and winced at the pain, but he wasn't going to let that stop him. He took a swig from the bottle of whiskey and didn't bother putting the cap back in.

He took a tentative step, then another, then started to work his way over to the window. When he reached the window, though, the leg really started to hurt—and there was another knock at the door.

EIGHT

"Come in!"

The door opened and a very attractive woman entered. She looked toward the bed, then around the room. Somebody had told her he'd be on the bed. Had the same person who sent the sheriff also sent her?

"Can I help you?" he asked.

She frowned at him and said, "Maybe I should be helping you?"

Clint could feel the sweat on his brow, hot and prickly.

"Well, I was trying to get a look out the window, but I guess it wasn't such a good idea."

"Would you like me to help you back to the bed?" she asked.

"I'd appreciate it."

She walked over, allowed him to lean on her, and helped him back to the bed. This time he was sitting on the other side of it, and it felt cool beneath him. After she straightened up, her perfume stayed with him.

"I thought I was taking root," he said.

"Are you in much pain? Would you like me to get the doctor?"

"No, no, I'll be fine."

"How about a drink?"

He looked over at the bottle and realized he'd drunk most of it.

"No, thanks. Um, was there something you wanted, Miss . . ."

"Oh, I'm sorry, Mr. Adams—"

"Clint," he said. "You saved me, so you get to call me Clint."

Now that she was closer he could see that she was perhaps five or six years older than he'd originally thought, forty, maybe forty-one, but very attractive. In fact, so attractive that he felt his body responding to her—to her and her scent.

"All right, Clint, my name is Mildred Haskell."

Mildred, he thought. The name did not fit her at all.

"Hello, Miss Haskell—or is it Mrs.?"

"It's Miss," she said, "but you may call me Mildred."

"All right, Mildred," he said, "what can I do for you?"

"Well, Mr.—Clint, it's not really what you can do for me, as much as what you could do for this town."

"For the town?"

She nodded.

"Tucumcari needs you," she said, so gravely that it was almost funny.

"To do what?"

"May I sit?" she asked, indicating the bed.

"Sure."

She sat next to him.

"We have our Founder's Day coming up next week— at the end of the week. It's actually ten days away."

"Uh-huh," he said. "I think I heard something about that."

"Well, we're having a fair surrounding the actual day, and we were trying to find a celebrity—"

"Celebrity?"

"Yes, a famous person—you know, like an actress, or a performer?"

"Yes," he said, "I know what a celebrity is, Mildred."

"Of course you do."

"And I'm not one."

She paused and stared at him.

"You're anticipating me."

"Maybe a little."

She put her hands in her lap primly, but she had already struck him as anything but a prim woman. He thought this was definitely an act.

"I'm doing this badly, aren't I?"

"I shouldn't have interrupted you," he said. "I'm sorry, you go ahead."

"Well, you know what I was going to ask you. Since you're here in Tucumcari, we were hoping that you'd be our celebrity."

"And what would your celebrity have to do?"

"Well . . . cut the ribbon."

"What ribbon?"

"We're going to have this ribbon, and having someone cut it is supposed to signify the birth of this town."

"Mildred," he said, "if I did that a lot of people would know I was here."

"Well, yes—"

"Do you have a newspaper?"

"Well, of course. The *Tucumcari Courier*."

"Well, the story would be in there, wouldn't it?"

"Yes—"

"You don't understand what I'm getting at, do you?" he asked.

"Well . . . I suppose not."

"With my reputation, as soon as the word got out that I was here it would attract certain . . . types."

"Types?"

"Men with guns, Mildred," Clint said. "Forgive me, but I think you're being deliberately dense here."

That seemed to insult her. She sat up straight and her prim demeanor went away.

"All right," she said, "I do know what you mean, but we have a sheriff—"

"Yes, I met your sheriff," Clint said. "He was here just before you . . . but I think you know that. Did you send him?"

"Of course not," she said. "He was probably just doing his job."

"Forgive me again, Mildred, but what do you do in town? Why were you the one to come and ask me?"

"I'm the mayor's secretary."

"Ah, I see. So you're here on his behalf?"

"I'm here on behalf of the town, Clint," she said. "Our Founder's Day could be a new beginning for this town."

"That may be, Mildred," Clint said, "but I don't think I can be part of it."

"Well," she said, standing up, "I think I'll leave and give you some time to think about it."

"I don't have to think about it, Mildred," Clint said. "For me to agree, I'd be making a target of myself."

"You can think about it, at least," she said. "I mean, what else do you have to do?"

He stared at her, then said, "I guess you're right about that, Mildred. What else do I have to do in Tucumcari?"

"We'll speak again, Clint," she said. "Please take good care of that leg."

"Oh, I will, Mildred," he said, "I will."

"That's all I ask, Clint," she said, "that's all I ask. Good day."

He watched her leave, and when she was gone her perfume was still in the air—and her effect was still there, too.

A very attractive woman.

NINE

"So?" Ed Biggers asked as Mildred Haskell entered his office.

She waited to reply until she had closed the door and seated herself.

"He won't do it."

"Why not?"

"The obvious reasons," she said. "He's afraid it will attract too much attention to him."

"To hell with him," Biggers said, "we *want* attention attracted to us."

Biggers stood up and walked to a map of the territory that was hanging on his wall.

"This could put us on the map at least, Mildred," he said. "Tucumcari could literally be on the map after this."

He tapped the map where Tucumcari would be if it was ever on the map.

"Well, he doesn't want to do it."

"How persuasive were you?"

"Well," she said, "I didn't sleep with him, if that's what you're asking."

"I was just asking you how persuasive you were," he

said. "Don't get up on your high horse about it."

"He's going to think it over."

"Well, that's good—"

"But he's not going to do it."

Biggers frowned.

"I don't like how convinced you sound."

"Sorry. This is not a man you can convince by appealing to his ego, and what do we have to offer him?"

"Publicity."

"You don't get it, Ed," she said. "He doesn't want publicity."

"Well . . ." Biggers said, looking at his map. He touched the spot where Tucumcari would be if it were on the map. He'd touched it so often there was a thumbprint there.

He turned and walked to his desk, then sat down.

"If he doesn't want publicity for himself, then we'll have to figure out a way to use him to get it for ourselves."

"And how do you plan on doing that?"

He regarded her over his pressed together palms, his index fingers just barely touching his nose, and said, "The Tucumcari Kid."

"You wouldn't."

"Who wants publicity even more than I do?" he asked.

"The Kid," she said, "but he doesn't want publicity, Ed, he wants a reputation."

"And he can get it through Clint Adams."

"He'd have to kill Adams to get it."

"I know," Biggers said, "or be killed."

"He doesn't get a reputation if *he's* killed by Clint Adams," she said, frowning.

"I know," Ed Biggers said, "but we would."

"So you'll let the Kid know that Clint Adams is here, and you don't care who kills who?"

"Well," Biggers said, "of course we get a bigger reputation and more publicity if Clint Adams is killed here."

"I don't believe you're saying this."

"Mildred, I don't want to be the mayor of a one-horse town forever."

"But this is not the way—"

"Then get Adams to cooperate," Biggers said. "It's up to you."

"That's not fair," she said. "That puts a lot of pressure on me."

"I know," he said, "but I've seen you perform under pressure before."

"Never anything of this magnitude."

"I have confidence that you will rise to the occasion, my dear."

"I don't think I like this side of you, Ed," she said, leaving the chair and walking to the door. "Not at all."

TEN

That evening Clint decided to try to get to the window again. There was a chair on the opposite side of the room, and he made a project of getting it to the window, so he'd be able to sit.

He got to his feet, limped to the wooden chair, then used it as a crutch to get to the window. That worked real well. He was then able to sit and look out at the street. He wondered if this little town with the long name might come to life at night. If it did, it would give him something to watch.

Unfortunately, it did not.

For one thing the room was on the side of the building. The window looked out on an alley, and it was only by craning his neck that he was able see a portion of the street.

Every so often he'd see someone go by, proof that there were other people around, but there wasn't anything near what you'd call foot traffic. Also, if there was a saloon in operation he couldn't hear it, not even when he opened the window. No piano, no voices talking or laughing or shouting, no gunshots, and no women.

Suddenly, he realized that he could smell food cooking and he was hungry. He'd made no provisions for food, and he certainly couldn't count on anyone coming to check on him. What if he starved to death in here? When would his body be found?

At that moment there was a knock on the door. He turned and eyed his gun on the bedpost, where he couldn't reach it. This would be a hell of a way to die, after all these years.

"Who is it?"

"It's Mildred Haskell. I've brought you some food."

Bless her heart.

"Come in."

She opened the door and entered, balancing a tray with a plate of food and a mug of beer on it. She looked around for a place to put it.

"On that table by the bed," he said. "Just move the bottle and the lamp."

She walked to the table, did as he asked, and set the tray down.

"I went to the café and asked them to donate some dinner."

"Donate?"

She smiled, turning to face him.

"Well, they do that sometimes when there's a prisoner in the jail."

"How often do you have prisoners in the jail?"

"Not often. I brought beer for you to drink, instead of whiskey."

"That's good," he said. "I prefer beer anyway."

"Would you like some help getting to the bed?"

"No," he said, "I came up with a system. Watch."

He stood up, then used the chair as a crutch again to get to the bed.

"See?"

"Very good. You know, I can go to Doc's, if you like, and see if he has an actual pair of crutches."

"That's okay," he said. "The chair is enough to get me around the room, and I don't think I'll be leaving for a while."

"Well, then," she said, "I'll leave you to your dinner."

"What should I do with the tray when I'm done?"

"Just leave it," she said. "I'll come by in the morning to collect it."

"Why are you doing this?" he asked. "I mean, I appreciate it and all, but why? Are you hoping to change my mind?"

"Well, yes, I am," she said. "Of course that's why I'm doing it. Why would I do it otherwise?"

"Maybe because you're a nice person?"

She seemed to give that some thought for a few moments, then shook her head and said, "Naw, I don't think so."

"Well, thanks anyway."

"I'll tell the desk clerk to come and check on you every so often to see if you need anything."

"I'd appreciate that," he said. "I neglected to make any plans, myself."

"That's understandable, Clint. Would you like me to have him bring breakfast to you in the morning?"

"A pot of coffee would be good."

"I'll take care of it."

"Thanks."

"Have a good night."

"You, too."

After she left he rolled to the other side of the bed

and looked at the food. It smelled good, and the beer looked wonderful. He tried that first. It had probably been cold when she started out, but it had warmed some. Still, it went down well.

Next he tried the beef stew, and while it wasn't the best he'd ever had, he was hungry enough not to complain. There were also some biscuits, which he used to soak up the last of the stew. When he was done he sat back with a half a mug of beer left and sipped it slowly, thoughtfully.

He'd never thought of himself as a celebrity before. Lillie Langtry, now there was a celebrity. Also Buffalo Bill Cody. But not him. He was just a man with a reputation. He just couldn't see himself presiding over any ribbon-cutting ceremony, not even in Tucumcari. It would just attract the wrong element. It wouldn't be good for him, and it wouldn't be good for the town.

Or would it?

Was he being too suspicious? Did the mayor, and the sheriff, and Mildred Haskell care *what* kind of publicity their Founder's Day attracted?

ELEVEN

Clint did not sleep well. He tossed and turned until the early hours when he finally did fall asleep. When he woke it was almost eleven a.m. He hadn't slept that late in a long time, and he didn't like the feeling. He wondered what had happened to the desk clerk with the coffee.

He was just sitting up, preparing to use the chair as a crutch, when there was a knock at the door. His gun was within easy reach so he called out for whoever it was to come in.

It was the desk clerk, Avery, and he had a pot of coffee and a mug.

"I thought you'd bring that by earlier," Clint said.

"I did," Avery said. "I knocked and you didn't answer. I figured you were asleep."

"What time was that?"

"About nine a.m. Do you want this?"

"Oh, yeah," Clint said, "I do. Look, I'm sorry. Thanks for bringing it by."

"Sure."

The clerk put it down on the night table next to the bed after picking up the tray.

"Want me to take this away?"

"I'd appreciate it. Thanks."

The clerk headed to the door.

"Hey, let me get you something."

"It's okay," Avery said. "Miss Haskell took care of me. I'll come look in on you in the afternoon."

"Okay, thanks."

Clint poured himself a cup of coffee as Avery closed the door. It was hot and black and that was all he required at the moment.

He was annoyed by what the clerk had told him. Sleeping too soundly was a good way to get killed. He couldn't believe that the man had knocked at nine a.m. and he hadn't heard a thing. He'd *never* slept that soundly before, not even when he'd been shot. Of course, the fact that he tossed and turned before finally falling asleep might have had something to do with it.

He finished his first cup of coffee and poured a second. From the size of the pot he figured he'd get six cups out of it. That suited him fine.

He sat back on the bed and drank the second cup more slowly. It occurred to him that his leg wasn't hurting so much now, probably because he'd been off it for hours. He looked over at the window. If he'd had a better view, there'd be a lot more reason to limp over to it. As it was, at that moment, it held little attraction for him.

He started to make a mental list of things he needed to make his stay more bearable. At the top of the list was a deck of cards. Further down he put some tools he'd need to clean his rifle and pistol. He might as well put the time to good use.

He could also use something to read. He remembered then that he had a book in his saddlebags, a new one for

him, a book of stories by Edgar Allan Poe. That solved
that problem.

He was on his fourth cup when he finished his mental
list. He could have used something to write it down on,
but he thought he'd remember most of it for whenever
the desk clerk came back, or maybe even Mildred Haskell.

Thinking of Mildred reminded him of something else
he thought he'd need while he was there. He wondered
if she'd be willing to give it to him.

TWELVE

The next person Clint saw was Mildred Haskell, which suited him just fine.

"I see you got your coffee," she said as she entered the room.

"Yes, thanks."

She walked to the pot and hefted it.

"Empty. I'll have it refilled. Would you like some lunch?"

"Sure."

"What would you like?"

"Anything will be fine."

"I'll be back within the hour."

"Mildred, could you bring me a paper and pencil? I'd like to make a list of things I need. I'm willing to pay for any of it."

"I'll bring the paper and pencil," she said. "That, at least, will be free."

"Thanks."

She left and returned in half an hour with more coffee, a sandwich, and the paper and pencil.

"I can wait while you make your list, unless you need more time."

"No, no," he said, "I know what I want."

He started writing the list, talking to her at the same time.

"I really feel bad taking advantage of you like this, Mildred."

"Like what?"

"Well, I'm turning you down for your Founder's Day and here you are waiting for me to write this list, and then you'll do your best to fill it . . . I just feel real guilty."

"Well," she said, smiling, "that's exactly my point, isn't it?"

"Is it?"

Still smiling, she asked, "Do you feel guilty enough to agree?"

Now he looked at her.

"No," he said, "I don't."

He handed her the list and she accepted it.

"I'll have someone bring these items to you, Clint."

"Thank you."

"I'll leave you to eat your lunch now."

"Thanks."

As she reached the door he called, "Mildred?"

"Yes?"

"Maybe when my leg heals we can have a real meal together?"

"Ask me again when it heals," she said, "and we'll see."

"I will."

After she left he ate his sandwich and washed it down with coffee. He was liking Mildred Haskell more and more. She seemed uncompromising and straight to the point. They both knew she was trying to make him feel

guilty, hoping he'd agree to be their ribbon-cutting celebrity on Founder's Day—but was that all she and the
others wanted?

He decided to ask the doctor about what was going
on, whenever he showed up to check on him. Maybe
he'd be more likely to talk plain about it.

As it turned out, the doctor came by late that afternoon. Clint was dead sure that his was the most knocked
on door in the hotel.

"Come in."

Doc Matthews entered with a smile on his weathered
face.

"How are you doing today, lad?"

"Doesn't hurt so much."

"You been staying off it?"

"Doesn't seem to be much reason to stand up on it,
Doc," Clint said.

"Let's have a look."

The doctor sat on the bed and probed Clint's leg with
practiced fingers.

"Swelling's startin' to go down. I see you been eatin'
well."

"I'm being taken care of," Clint said. "Doc, did you
know about this Founder's Day thing?"

Without looking up, Matthews said, "I know about
Founder's Day, of course. What exactly do you mean?"

"I mean do you know that a woman named Mildred
Haskell has been after me to be some kind of celebrity
for the thing?"

"Mildred can be very persuasive."

"I know that."

"So you've agreed?"

"I have not," Clint said. "It's not good for a man with my reputation to announce his presence anywhere, Doc, let alone a Founder's Day celebration."

"So you turned her down, eh?" Doc looked up at Clint when he asked this.

"You knew about this, didn't you? Wait a minute. I get it now. You're the one who told them about me. You told—let me guess—you told the mayor, and he sent his secretary over to ask me."

"I didn't see the harm," Matthews said, "seein' as how you'd be here and all."

"If I didn't know better, Doc," Clint said, "I'd swear you lied about my leg being fractured just to keep me here."

"Oh, it's fractured all right, you can count on that."

"I can feel that," Clint said, "or I'd be out of here already."

"You can't be complainin' about seein' Mildred," Doc said.

"Mildred's real pretty, Doc, and I like her, and she's taking real good care of me, but the answer's still going to be no."

"That's between you and her, I guess," Doc said, standing up.

"And the mayor," Clint said. "Don't forget the mayor. When do I get a visit from him so he can ask me himself?"

"I can't speak for the mayor, lad," Matthews said. "If he wants to come by and see you he will. I got to go now. I got other patients."

Clint doubted that. How many patients could he have in Tucumcari?

"Okay, Doc," Clint said. "When will I be seeing you again?"

"Oh, I'll check up on you tomorrow," Matthews said. "Meantime I guess Mildred will be in and out."

"I'm sure she will," Clint said. "Also, the desk clerk's been real nice about checking to see if I need anything."

"Yep," Matthews said, "Tucumcari's a real friendly town."

Sure, Clint thought as the Doc left, when they want something from you.

THIRTEEN

Mike Black couldn't imagine what Mayor Ed Biggers would want with him. Black knew for a fact that Biggers wouldn't cross the street to piss on him if he was on fire—unless he thought it would help him politically. So what did he want to talk to him about now?

Black entered the city hall building and stopped when he saw Mildred Haskell. He knew that Mildred was more than a dozen years older than him, but she was a fine-looking woman just the same. Like most of the men in town, Mike Black was smitten with her.

"Hello, Mildred."

She looked up from her desk and smiled when she saw him. He was holding his hat, turning it and crushing it in his hands.

"Well, hello, Mike. How are you?"

"I'm fine, I guess," he said. "Uh, I heard Ed—uh, Mayor Biggers wanted to see me."

"Yes, he does," she said, leaning forward and drawing him into her lovely violet eyes. "He needs your help with something *very* important."

"Me?"

Black was tall and thin, almost emaciated. He ate

maybe one meal a day and he never finished that. He supplemented his food intake with beer and whiskey, and he smoked like a steam engine. His teeth were yellowed, as were the tips of his fingers and the corners of his mouth. He was not an attractive man, but right at that moment he felt like he was the center of Mildred Haskell's universe—and he liked the feeling.

"You will help, won't you, Mike?"

"Sure," Black said, "if I can."

"I think you can," she said. "Why don't you go on in and see the mayor, huh? He'll explain it all to you."

"Sure, Mildred," Black said, "whatever you say."

Before Mike Black entered his office, Mayor Ed Biggers was thinking about the man. As distasteful as he found even being in the same town with the man, let alone the same room, Mike Black had something nobody else had.

He had the ear of the Tucumcari Kid, and at the moment, that was a very important commodity.

He looked up just as Mike Black entered his office. He could tell from the look on his face that Mildred had done her job of softening him up.

"Hello, Mike."

"Uh, hello, Mayor," Black said. "I heard you wanted to see me."

"Yes, I do, Mike," Biggers said, standing up. "I need your help, Mike. The town needs your help."

"What can I do?"

"Have you ever heard of Clint Adams?"

Black's eyes widened.

"You mean, the Gunsmith?"

"That's who I mean."

"Well, sure," Black said, "everybody's heard of him. He's the most famous gunman since Hickok."

"He's here."

"Where?" Black actually looked around, as if Clint Adams were in the same room with them. Biggers wondered how a man could be so stupid.

"He's in town."

"Oh." Black relaxed.

"He's at the hotel, and he's going to be in town for a while."

"Why?"

"Well, he was passing through and it seems he got kicked by a horse. He has a fractured leg."

Black frowned.

"What do you want me to do?"

"Mike, I want you to keep an eye on him."

"What for?"

"Because you know what having that kind of man in town could do."

"I do? What?"

Biggers closed his eyes for a moment, took a deep breath, and then opened them.

"He can cause trouble, Mike," he said patiently, "and we don't want any trouble in Tucumcari, do we?"

"No, we sure don't," Black said. Then he added, "What kind of trouble?"

"What would happen, Mike, if, say, the Kid found out Adams was here?"

"Oh," Black said. Then his eyes widened and he said, "Oh!" again.

"You see what I mean," Biggers said. "If the Kid heard about Adams, why he'd be back here like a shot, wouldn't he?"

"He sure would."

"And what would happen?"

"He'd kill Adams."

"Or Adams would kill him."

"Uh-uh," Black said. "The Kid's the fastest I ever seen."

"Really?" Biggers asked. "You think the Kid could take Clint Adams?"

"Uh-huh!"

"Well," Biggers said, "we wouldn't want that to happen, would we?"

"We wouldn't?"

"Of course not."

"Why not?"

"What would happen to the Kid if he killed Clint Adams?" Biggers asked.

Black thought a moment, then said, "He'd be big. He'd be the biggest man in this county."

"The country," Biggers said. "He'd be the biggest man in this country, Mike. The man who killed Clint Adams."

"Yeah!"

"And he'd have to live with that reputation."

"Yeah!" Black said again, his eyes becoming big as saucers.

"So I want you to keep your eye on Clint Adams," Biggers said, "and make sure that the Kid doesn't find out he's here. Can you do that for me, Mike?"

"I sure can, Mayor."

"Good man," Biggers said. He contemplated walking around the desk and patting Black on the back, but he couldn't bring himself to touch the man. "I knew we could count on you."

"You sure can," Mike Black said, and he left the office like his ass was on fire.

Ed Biggers sat down behind his desk and smiled.

He was still smiling when Mildred came in a short time later.

"He's going to go right to the Kid," she said.

"I know."

She shook her head.

"I have to go, Ed," she said. "I have to get a few things for Clint Adams."

"You do that, Mildred," he said. "You keep our guest real happy while he's here."

"Yeah," she said, "I'll do that, Ed."

When she left him, Mayor Ed Biggers was still sitting in his chair, his hands behind his head, smiling.

FOURTEEN

When Mildred returned to Clint's room she had help in bringing him the things he needed. She had apparently grabbed Jake from the livery, and they both entered Clint's room with the things on his list.

"Thanks for your help, Jake," she said.

From the look on Jake's face it was obvious that Clint didn't have to toss him the price of a drink this time. He'd been only too happy to help Mildred.

"My pleasure, ma'am," Jake said, and left.

"I just needed some help carrying some of the things," she told Clint.

"Did you get the most important item?" he asked, looking at the pile of things she'd dumped on the dresser top.

"Yes," she said, "the instruments you need to clean your weapons?"

"No," he said, "the cards."

"Oh, those," she said. She dug into the pile and came up with two sealed decks. She tossed them to him one at a time and he caught them.

"Thanks."

"Are you a gambler?"

"I like poker," he said. "There wouldn't be a game in town somewhere that you'd know about?"

She started to say no, but then an idea occurred to her. "I might be able to arrange something."

"Oh," he said, "if I agree—"

"No, no," she said, "nothing like that. Just let me talk to a few people and get back to you."

"I appreciate it—and thanks for all the things."

"No problem," she said. "I hope it all helps to pass the time."

"Maybe . . ." he said and paused.

"Yes?"

"I just thought . . . maybe you'd like to help me pass some of the time."

She smiled and asked, "What did you have in mind?"

"Well, I thought . . . you know . . . that maybe we could have dinner in here one night."

She hesitated, then said, "That sounds interesting. I'll consider it."

"Good."

"Was the doctor here today?"

"Yeah, he was."

"What did he say?"

"I'm coming along."

"Good," she said, "good."

There was an awkward moment that passed between them, and then she backed toward the door.

"I guess I'll get going. I'll stop by later."

"Thanks, Mildred."

"Sure, Clint," she said. "Anytime."

After she left he wondered if she had known what he *really* meant when he asked about her helping him to pass the time. Yeah, she must have. Whether she was thirty-nine, forty, or forty-one, she'd been around. She knew what a man wanted from her.

He cracked the seal on one of the decks of cards and started dealing out a hand of solitaire on the bed. It was amazing how comforting a deck of cards could be in your hands. All of a sudden he had something to do, and it made all the difference.

Mildred Haskell thought about Clint's request as she walked down the hall. Dinner in his room, and what else? She was sure she knew what he had in mind. It was what most men thought when they saw her, and she took no offense from it. Men had looked at her that way all her life, and at her age she probably should appreciate it even more. After all, at forty-five how many more years of it did she have?

Besides, Clint Adams was an extremely interesting man, and there was a mighty big shortage of those in Tucumcari.

FIFTEEN

Mike Black didn't know what to do.

Ed Biggers had told him to keep an eye on Clint Adams, but he also felt obligated to his friend, the Tucumcari Kid, to let him know that Adams was in town. Black knew that this was an opportunity that the Kid would not want to pass up.

Black was standing across the street from the hotel. He'd gone inside to talk to Avery, but all he could find out about Adams was what room he was in. Avery wouldn't say anything beyond that and seemed scared to talk about the man at all.

Mike Black himself would have been scared, too, if he wasn't such good friends with the Tucumcari Kid. He'd seen the Kid in action, and there was no way anyone could be faster than him with a gun, not even the Gunsmith. Besides, the Gunsmith was so *old* now, and the Kid wasn't even twenty-five yet.

So he stood across from the hotel wondering how he was going to get word to the Kid. He was using his brain more than he ever had before, and he swore it was giving him a headache.

• • •

Mildred saw Mike Black standing in a doorway across from the hotel when she left and smiled to herself. Ed Biggers had outsmarted himself this time. How was Black going to get word to the Kid about Adams if he had to stay in town and watch him? There was no telegraph in Tucumcari—something else that Biggers was working on—so the only way Black was going to get word to the Kid was to leave town and find him. Could the man even figure that out for himself?

Briefly she considered going across and suggesting it to him. After all, with a fractured leg where was Clint Adams going to go?

In the end she decided to leave Mike Black to his own devices, and she headed back to the office.

Black watched as Mildred left the hotel. He knew that she had brought Adams some stuff because he couldn't get around with his leg broke.

Then it hit him.

If Adams couldn't go anywhere, then where was the harm in leaving town just long enough to get to the Kid? The next town, Benton, had a telegraph office. He just needed to get there, send a telegram, and get back. Adams had just broke his leg yesterday, so there was no way he could leave the hotel.

Feeling real proud of himself, Mike Black started for the livery.

SIXTEEN

Harvey Little hated his name.

As soon as he was old enough he tried to change it. He wanted people to stop calling him "Little Harvey," but being short didn't help. Nobody took him seriously—until the day he picked up a gun for the first time. It felt so right in his hand, like nothing else he'd ever held, not even his mother's hand.

After that he found out that he was a natural with a handgun. He could hit anything he pointed it at, no matter what the size of the target was. His only limitation was in distance. To try to overcome that he picked up a rifle, but it wasn't the same thing. No matter how much he practiced he just wasn't as good with the long gun as he was with the short. Finally, he gave up and decided to be satisfied with what he could do with the short one.

He started carrying the gun in his belt when he was fourteen and didn't get a holster until three years later. It didn't matter, though. Holster or belt, he could still get the gun out faster than anyone had ever seen before. People started to respect him then, or maybe fear him. Whatever the reason, though, they stopped calling him "Little Harvey" and even stopped calling him "Harvey.'' Instead, they called him by the name he had picked out for himself.

The Tucumcari Kid.

He was eighteen the first time he was called the ''Kid,'' and that was seven years ago. Over those years he had killed a lot of men in fair gunfights and made a name for himself in New Mexico.

When Mike Black's telegram found him, the Tucumcari Kid was in a whorehouse in Bevins, New Mexico.

The whore's name was Angela. She was a darkskinned, raven-haired, big-breasted girl who stood about five eight or nine—which made her a good five inches taller than the Kid.

The Kid liked big women. He knew they wouldn't give him a second look if he wasn't who he was, and he always made sure he introduced himself. He was a regular at a lot of the whorehouses in the county now, and this particular whore, Angela, was a favorite of his. She had learned a long time ago what his favorite thing to do was, and she always did it.

He liked having a girl her size sit astride him, his hard penis rammed up inside of her, talking to him in Spanish while she rode him. Then, when he was almost ready to finish, he'd push her off and she'd go down there with her hands and her mouth. She'd suck him until he was almost ready to explode, then would do something with her fingers that would stop him. After that she'd come up and sit on him again and they'd start over. She'd do this, up and down, back and forth, a few times until he'd finally explode, sometimes deep up inside of her, and other times in her mouth.

She didn't care which. She was getting paid either way.

On this day he finished in her mouth, and she closed her nails over his buttocks and sucked him dry.

"Hoo, girl," he said, as she released him from her mouth, "that was something."

"You like when Angela does that to you, eh, *jefe*?" she said sweetly, lying down beside him.

"I love it when you do that to me, baby."

She laughed and drew her red nails over his belly and up over his chest.

"You just let me rest a bit," he said, "and then we'll—"

He was interrupted by a knock at the door.

"Who the hell is that?"

"There's a telegram for you," a voice called.

"Bring it in."

The door opened and a young girl entered. She was maybe fifteen and pretty, and he recognized her. Her name was Rosa, and she worked in the whorehouse, although not as a whore. She was young and pretty and probably would be a whore one of these days, but not yet. When she was, maybe he'd ask for her. She wasn't big like the other women he liked; she was more his size, and she was *very* pretty.

He knew that she delivered messages, and kept the house clean for the madam, and did the laundry for the other girls.

"This is for you," she said, holding the telegram in her hand.

"Bring it here, darlin'," he said.

Shyly she approached the bed, averting her eyes from their nakedness.

"Why are you so shy?" the Kid asked.

"She is young, *chico*," Angela said to him, "too young for you to concern yourself with. I am all the woman you need."

Angela gave Rosa a gloating look and ran her hand down to the Kid's genitals. She stroked him until he started to become hard again.

"Stop that!" he snapped at her.

He grabbed the telegram from Rosa, who then turned and ran from the room.

Angela rolled away from him, crossing her arms over her big breasts, pouting, but the Kid ignored her and read the badly composed telegram from Mike Black.

SEVENTEEN

"He wants to what?" Ed Biggers asked.

"Play poker."

"In his room?"

No, Mildred thought, that's not what he wants to do in his room.

"Probably not."

"I don't play poker," Biggers said.

"Does anyone in town play?"

"I don't know," he said, annoyed. "Jesus, sitting around a table throwing your money away. What a way to spend your life."

"He doesn't want to spend his life doing it," Mildred said, "just a few days. Besides, I understand some people actually win."

"I don't think—"

"You want to keep him in a good mood, don't you?" she asked. "I mean, you don't want him to leave town, do you?"

Biggers squared his jaw.

"Find him somebody to play with, then," he said finally.

"I'll talk to Doc," she said. "I understand he used to play."

"Do that," Biggers said. "Talk to Doc."

As Mildred left the mayor's office, Biggers sat back and rubbed his hands over his face. They were going to have to keep Adams entertained in order to keep him in town until the Kid decided to come in. That was the thing about the Tucumcari Kid. You never knew what he was going to do, or when he was going to do it.

Biggers hated that he had to depend on men like Clint Adams and the Tucumcari Kid to make this Founder's Day thing work.

Mildred walked to the doctor's office and found the old man sitting behind his desk.

"What are you doing, Doc?" she asked.

He looked at her with blue eyes that were not as clear as they used to be.

"I thought if I sat still long enough," he explained, "I might just . . . stop."

"Stop?"

He nodded.

"You mean . . . die?"

"I just thought it might be time."

"I guess you were wrong."

"I guess so," he said. He looked directly at her then, and she thought she saw his blue eyes twinkle. Was he joking with her?

"What can I do for you, Mildred?"

"You used to play poker, didn't you?"

"Yes," he said, "I used to."

"But you still know how, don't you?"

"I still know the rules, yes."

"Does anyone else in town play?"

He frowned.

"I suppose so. What's this all about?"

"Clint wants to play."

"Clint Adams?"

"Yes."

"He wants to play poker."

"Yes."

Doc Matthews smiled.

"And Ed wants to keep him happy, right?"

"Yes."

"Poker," Doc said thoughtfully, "hmm . . . who plays poker in town?"

"Why don't you think about it and let me know, Doc?" Mildred asked.

"I could go over to the saloon and find somebody."

"I don't think he'd settle for just anybody, Doc," Mildred said. "See if you can find some good players."

"In Tucumcari?" Doc Matthews asked.

Mildred headed for the door and said, "Do the best you can, will you . . . and don't die?"

Matthews smiled and said, "I'll do my best."

When she left he was sitting motionless behind his desk, as he had when she entered.

She hoped he *was* joking with her.

EIGHTEEN

When the knock came Clint thought that maybe he should just be leaving the door wide open.

"Come in."

The door opened and Doc Matthews came in.

"Back so soon?" Clint asked.

"Why not?" Matthews asked. "You're my only patient, at the moment."

"Maybe business will pick up."

"I hope not," Matthews said, approaching the bed. "I'm semiretired."

Matthews checked Clint's leg again and the condition hadn't changed since he'd looked at it earlier in the day.

"Comin' along," the doctor said.

"Why don't you tell me why you're really here, Doc?" Clint asked. "Did the mayor send you?"

"No."

"Mildred."

"Well . . ."

"Why?"

"She said something about you wanting to play some poker."

"Are you a poker player, Doc?"

"I was, a long time ago."

"And are there any other players in town?"

"Not really."

"So what did you think we'd do?" Clint asked. "Play two-handed for a while?"

Doc Matthews frowned.

"Wait a minute," Clint said.

"What?"

"We could do that."

"Play two-handed?"

"Sure," Clint said. "You just said you have no other patients, and I certainly have nothing else to do."

Matthews looked on the floor next to the bed, where Clint's rifle was lying, partially stripped for cleaning.

"I can do that anytime," Clint said. "What do you say?"

"Where would we play? On the bed?"

"We could get Avery to bring in a table and another chair. It wouldn't have to be a big table."

"But . . . I haven't played in years. What would we play for?"

"Bring some chips and we'll play . . . we'll play for your bill."

"What?"

"Your bill," Clint said. "You said you were going to bill me. We'll each take some chips. Whatever I win you deduct from your bill, and whatever you win we'll add to it."

Doc was quiet.

"We can also talk," Clint added, thinking that maybe the older man had no one to talk to. "You can tell me about the people here in Tucumcari. What do you say, Doc?"

"Well," Doc said, "it would give me something to do."

"Great," Clint said, excited by the prospect of a two-handed poker game. "Why don't you go get the chips and talk to Avery about the table."

"Right now?"

"Now's as good a time as any, Doc."

"I guess you're right," Doc Matthews said. "All right. I'll be back soon."

"I'll be right here."

Not normally something a man would get excited about, this two-handed game in the offing had both men in that state of mind.

Clint was excited because he was going to have something to do, and somebody to talk to.

Doc was excited because lately he'd been feeling lonely and useless. This would also give him something to do, and Clint was willing to talk to him. The latter was even more exciting than the former.

When Doc returned with the chips, he also had Avery with him. The desk clerk carried in a small wooden table and set it up by the window, then went out and got another chair.

"You fellas need anything else?" he asked.

"I got everything else we need," Doc said. "Thanks, Avery."

As Avery left Doc put the chips on the table, then pulled a bottle of whiskey out of his pocket.

"Just to wet our whistles."

"Sounds good to me, Doc."

Clint used his chair to limp over to the table.

"You remind me when you're healed some," Doc said, seated across from him, "I've got some crutches in my office you can use when you start walkin' again."

"You better hold on to those crutches, Doc," Clint said, shuffling the cards while Doc counted out their chips.

"Why's that, lad?"

"You just might need to bet them."

"Is that a fact?"

"Five-card stud all right with you?" Clint asked.

"Son," Doc said, "that was always my game."

"Fine," Clint said, dealing the first three cards. "King to you, and queen to the dealer. Your bet, Doc."

NINETEEN

They played poker all afternoon, and then Doc had to get up and move around.

"I'll go and get some food," he said.

"Bring it back here and we can eat together," Clint said. "I still want to hear some more about your local politics."

Doc laughed.

"Local politics around here has been Ed Biggers for twenty years."

"And Mildred."

"She's been with Ed all that time."

"She's from here, then?"

"Born and raised," Doc said. "I delivered her. In fact, she was one of the first babies I delivered hereabouts. God, I was young then."

"Go and get that dinner, Doc. I want to hear more."

"Café's got a good beef stew," Doc said, "and I'll bring back some beer."

"I'll be waiting."

Clint felt better than he had all day. Concentrating on poker, and on Doc's stories, was keeping his mind off his leg.

Under normal circumstances the stories might not have been so interesting, but Doc's intensity when he was talking almost made up for it.

"Folks round here got tired of hearin' me talk a long time ago," Doc had explained.

"Well, Doc," Clint had said, "I'm a captive audience, so you just go ahead and talk up a storm."

He talked about the boot maker's wife and what a tough delivery she'd had back in '58, about the time he had to dig a foot-long splinter out of old Deke Peters back in '66, and on and on about other patients he'd had over the past forty years. Clint listened in rapt attention and asked questions now and again.

As for the poker, Clint was just playing to pass the time, so even when he felt he had a strong hand he didn't push it, and once or twice he'd even folded a winning hand on purpose. After all, if Doc kept losing he might get tired of playing.

Then somewhere along the way the game probably came back to Doc Matthews and he started playing better, started winning enough so that Clint had to start to concentrate.

It was all more fun than Clint ever thought it would be. Of course, that scared him and made him long for the day when he could leave Tucumcari, but at least he had something to do until then. He had an idea that Doc wouldn't run out of stories even by the time he was ready to leave.

Doc returned with a tray bearing two bowls of beef stew, some biscuits, and a couple of beers. He was huffing and puffing from the effort when he finally got there, but proudly announced that he hadn't spilled a drop.

They cleared the table so they could eat, and Clint told Doc to keep on talking.

"What was I talking about?" the older man asked.

"Mildred Haskell."

"Ah, Mildred," Doc said, his eyes lighting up. "You should have seen her when she was younger, Clint. Good God, she was a beauty."

"She's not so bad right now, Doc," Clint said.

"Oh, I know, but she's more a handsome figure of a woman now. In her twenties, even her thirties, she was a raving beauty."

"Why did she stay here, Doc? A woman that beautiful, sounds like she could have moved on."

"She's loyal, that's why."

"Loyal to the town?"

"To the town," Doc said, "and to Mayor Ed Biggers."

"Is there something going on between them?" Clint asked. "Something more than secretary and boss?"

"If you ask me," Doc said, "and if you ask Ed's wife and a lot of other people around here the answer's yes, but nobody can prove it."

"What's the mayor like?"

"He's ten or twelve years older than her and as homely as—well, as homely as a man can get."

"What's the attraction, then?"

"He's smart."

"That's it?"

"There aren't too many smart men in these parts, Clint."

"You're here, Doc."

"I'm a doctor," he said, "that don't necessarily make me smart."

"Smarter than most."

"Not as smart as Ed Biggers."

"Okay then, what's he doing here if he's so smart?"

Doc Matthews washed down his food with a mouthful of beer and then looked straight at Clint.

"Let me tell you something about Tucumcari, lad," he said. "This is home to some people. Not a lot of people, mind you, but some. Not everybody feels that they're trapped here. Ed Biggers has been trying for twenty years to get this town on the map. Some of us think he'll do it one of these days."

"I'm sorry, Doc," Clint said after a moment. "I guess I shouldn't be so quick to judge, huh?"

"I guess not."

They finished their dinner after that, then cleared the table for poker.

By the time Doc had had enough for the night, Clint had won back about half the physician's fee.

"The game's coming back to you, Doc," Clint said.

"I'll get it back tomorrow."

"After lunch?"

"I'll be here."

TWENTY

Clint slept better that night than he had the night before, and woke refreshed. Avery brought him a pot of coffee at nine a.m. and removed the remnants of his and Doc's shared meal from the night before.

"How's the game goin'?" he asked.

"Not bad," Clint said. "Doc's a little ahead."

"Wish I could play."

"Do you know how?"

"Oh, yeah," Avery said, "I know how, I just ain't got the money—"

"We can work something out, Avery," Clint said. "I'm just looking to pass the time. We're not playing for high stakes. Would you like to play?"

"Well, sure."

"When do you get off work today?"

"At four."

"Come on by then," Clint said, "and bring another chair."

"Gee, thanks, Mr. Adams."

"If we're going to be playing poker together," Clint said, "call me Clint."

"Sure thing, Clint."

Avery left, pleased to have been invited, and Clint was happy to have a third hand in the game.

It was Mildred who brought his lunch. As she entered she looked at the table curiously.

"Got a poker game going," Clint said.

"With who?"

"Doc," he said. "Yesterday it was just Doc, but today Avery's going to play."

"Avery?"

Clint nodded as she put his sandwich and a fresh pot of coffee down.

"You look happy."

"Happy's a strong word," Clint said, "but I'm in a better mood."

"How's the leg?"

"Hurts some," Clint said, "but it's not bad. At least I'm playing poker with my doctor, so if anything goes wrong, he'll be here."

"Mind if I sit a minute?" she asked.

"No, please go ahead."

She went to the table and sat while Clint bit into the sandwich.

"When is he coming back?" she asked.

"After lunch."

"Has he been talking your ear off?" she asked. "Doc doesn't get much chance to talk to people these days."

"So he told me," Clint said. "He's filling me in on the town history."

"Is he?"

"Oh, yeah. I know who broke what bone and when, and who had a tough delivery—I even know that he delivered you."

"He told you that, did he? What else did he tell you, I wonder?"

"He told me you were the prettiest baby he ever delivered."

"Either he's a liar or you are," she said. "I was an ugly baby."

"But look at you now."

She looked down at her folded hands.

"Thank you, but there was a time . . ." She shook her head and stood up. "I have to go."

"Did you think about my invitation?"

"I did," she said, "but it looks like you'll have a full house here tonight. Maybe tomorrow night?"

"I'll kick these bums out, for sure," he said, "that's a promise."

"Then I'll be here."

"It's a date, then. Will you arrange for the food? We even have a table now."

"Yes," she said, "I'll take care of the food."

"Then I'll see you tomorrow night."

"Oh," she said, "you'll probably see me before then. Take care of your leg, and don't let Doc and Avery win all your money."

"I'll try not to."

She left and he finished his sandwich and waited impatiently for Doc to arrive for their game.

Mildred left the hotel and hurried back to the office to talk to Biggers. Doc was a talker, all right, and he knew everything there was to know about everyone in town—herself, the mayor, and the Tucumcari Kid.

TWENTY-ONE

"What the hell could he be telling him?" Ed Biggers asked Mildred.

"I don't know, Ed," she said, "but we know how he likes to talk."

"What if he tells him about the Kid?" Biggers asked. "What if Adams decides to leave town?"

"You think he'd be scared of the Kid?"

"No," Biggers said, "I guess not. He's the Gunsmith, after all."

"Besides, he can't ride," Mildred said. "I don't think we have to worry about him leaving for a while."

"Well, then, let the old man talk," Biggers said. "After all, what can he tell him that could hurt us?"

"Nothing, I guess," Mildred said, but somehow Mayor Biggers didn't look all that convinced.

Doc arrived, ready to play and ready to talk. They were two hours into the game when he finally brought up the Tucumcari Kid.

"The what?"

"If we have a local celebrity," Doc said, "it's the Kid."

"Who named him that?"

"He did," Doc said. "Seems he hated his real name."

"Which was?"

"I probably shouldn't be tellin' you this," Doc said, "but I don't guess you'll be meetin' him. It's Harvey, Harvey Little. When he was growin' up folks used to call him—"

"Let me guess," Clint said. "Little Harvey?"

"That's right," Doc said.

"You got an ace, Doc. Your bet."

"Two bits," Doc said, tossing in a white chip.

"Call."

"Used to get him mad as hell, especially since he didn't grow up to be more than five foot four."

"How did he get to be a local celebrity?"

"He picked up a gun."

"No."

"That's what happened. He picked up a gun and damned if he wasn't a natural with it."

"Two aces, Doc."

"Half a dollar."

"Call," Clint said. "A natural shot?"

"And a natural killer."

Clint shook his head.

"I've known a lot of kids like that. I haven't ever heard of him, though."

"He stays in New Mexico," Doc said. "He claims to have killed twenty men. Hot damn, a third ace."

"Can't beat that hand, Doc. I fold. How old is he?"

"About twenty-five," Doc said, raking in his chips and then gathering the cards together to shuffle.

"He's probably lying," Clint said. "Did you deliver him, too?"

"Oh, yeah," Doc said. "Delivered most of the folks around here."

"Does he come to town often?"

"Once in a while—oh." Doc paused in his dealing and looked at Clint with a concerned expression.

"What is it?"

"Well, if he comes to town while you're here he won't be able to resist challenging you."

"I'm in no position to accept any challenges, Doc, as you know."

"That won't matter to the Kid," Doc said. "He tends to make his own rules."

"Well, not with me."

"He's very good, Clint," Doc said, leaning on the table. "I don't know for sure how many men he's killed, but I know he's killed some. He can hit anything with a pistol, and he's fast."

"Are you warning me, Doc?"

"I'm just making you aware, lad," Doc Matthews said. "If he comes to town you'll have to contend with him."

"Why don't we just wait and see if that happens, huh, Doc? Why don't you deal."

TWENTY-TWO

Later that afternoon, when they took a break, Clint told Doc that Avery would be joining them at four o'clock.

"Good," Doc said, "a third hand will make the game interesting."

"That's what I was thinking."

"I'll come back at four then," Doc said. "That's a half hour from now. I should be rested."

"Hey, Doc?"

"Yes?" Matthews turned before he reached the door.

"How old are you, anyway?"

"Old enough to teach you something about poker, young fella," Doc said and left.

Clint hoped that the long poker sessions wouldn't take their toll on the man. He was starting to enjoy his company.

At four o'clock there was a knock on the door, and Clint called out for Avery to come in.

"Where's Doc?" Avery asked.

"He'll be along shortly," Clint said. "Did you bring another chair?"

"Got it right here."

Avery brought the chair in from the hall and set it at the table.

For a few moments they went over what Avery knew about poker. Clint discovered that the man had the rudiments of the game, he just never got much of a chance to play. They played a few hands while they waited for Doc, and Clint once again assured Avery that the stakes were low.

"Here are your chips," Clint said, and went over the three different colors with him.

"What happens if I lose them all?" Avery asked nervously.

"Don't worry about it," Clint said. "Doc and I have our own arrangement. I'm sure we can come to an agreement about what you're playing for."

Doc entered then without knocking, and for that Clint was grateful.

"Ah, our new player is here. Excellent."

Doc sat down and picked up the cards happily.

"We'll have to figure out what Avery's playing for, Doc."

"No problem," Doc said.

"As long as it ain't a lot of money," Avery said.

"These are just chips, lad," Doc said, "not money. We're just trying to keep our new friend, here, from going crazy, that's all."

"And I appreciate it, fellas," Clint said. "Doc, deal the cards."

TWENTY-THREE

Across the street Mike Black wondered what was going on in Clint Adams's room. What if he'd somehow gone out the back door of the hotel? What if he was gone? How would the mayor react? And what about the Kid?

Black decided that since Adams's room was on the ground floor he'd better risk a look in the window. He left his doorway and crossed the street. When he got there he went to the alley and worked his way to the window of Clint Adams's room. When he looked inside he was both relieved and surprised. He was relieved that the man was still there, but surprised that both Doc and Avery, the desk clerk, were playing poker with him.

Black watched from the window, wishing he could join the game.

In his office Sheriff Caleb York was stewing. He'd been embarrassed during his talk with Clint Adams, and he was desperately trying to think of a way to make up for it.

He'd been instructed to stay away from Adams, but he decided to at least go across to the hotel and see what was going on. After all, he was the law, wasn't he? He had a right to check on strangers in town.

He got up from his desk, grabbed his hat, and left, heading for the hotel.

Mildred Haskell sat at her desk and wondered what she was going to do about Clint Adams. She was strongly attracted to the man, and she knew he felt the same way, so she knew that she was going to have sex with him. That wasn't the problem. The problem was what to tell him, if anything, about what was going on.

The problem, when you got right down to it, was whether or not to tell him about the Tucumcari Kid.

Of course, if Doc Matthews had already told him, that would solve the problem. So what she needed to find out from the good doctor was just how much talking he'd been doing with Mr. Adams.

"Ed?" she asked, going to Biggers's door.

"Yeah?"

"Do you need me for anything?"

"No, why?"

"I have to go out."

"Well, go ahead. I'm done here. I'll be going home soon."

"Give Ethel my best."

"Yeah," he said sourly.

Mildred locked her desk and left the office.

After Mildred left, Ed Biggers got up and walked to the map on his wall. He touched the smudged fingerprint he'd been leaving there all these years. He changed the map every so often, especially when boundaries were changed, but he always tried to keep an up-to-date map on the wall, and a clean one, at that. Still, after a few weeks that smudged fingerprint was always there because *that's* where Tucumcari was going to be as soon as he succeeded in getting it put on the damn map.

He turned and went back to his desk. Twenty years he'd been the mayor of this town, and what did he have to show for it? This was going to be his last chance. If he couldn't use Clint Adams to secure Tucumcari a place in the county, then he was going to give up. Ethel had been after him to leave this place for ten years now, and he was just about ready. The only thing he didn't know was who he was going to take with him, Ethel or Mildred.

Who was he kidding?

He sat down heavily in his chair, the same chair he'd had all these years. It was like him, though, tired and showing cracks and creases, but like him it would always be here. Here he was mayor, and even without a place on the map, people looked up to him. If he left, where would he go? What could he do? Start over at fifty-eight years of age? He doubted it.

He pulled out his pocket watch and regarded it. It was past six. Ethel would be wondering where he was. She'd probably scream at him for being with Mildred, and this time he wasn't. He heaved himself out of his chair, grabbed his hat, and left the office. He intended to go home, but maybe he'd stop off at the hotel first. It was time he had a talk of his own with Clint Adams.

In Bevins the Tucumcari Kid was lying with Angela, but he was thinking about Tucumcari, the place where he was born, where people had made fun of him until he'd discovered the gun. He'd sent Mike Black a telegram in return, telling him that he'd be coming home soon. He didn't say when, though, because he wasn't sure. For one thing, he wasn't sure he wanted to go back there. He hadn't been home in months, and he had just about decided that he never wanted to go back, and now this.

Ah well, a chance at Clint Adams, the Gunsmith, that was a strong lure. That was too good to pass up.

Tomorrow morning he'd start riding for Tucumcari. He knew that Ed Biggers had been trying to get the town on the county map for years.

It looked like they were both going to get their big chance.

TWENTY-FOUR

Mike Black started when he heard something behind him in the alley. He turned and saw Sheriff York coming toward him.

"What the hell are you doin' here, Mike?" York demanded.

"I'm watchin'."

"Watchin' what?"

Instead of answering Black just pointed, and York looked in the window.

"What are they doin'?" he asked. "Playin' poker?"

"That's what they're doin'."

"But . . . why?"

Black shrugged.

York looked in the window again. He saw Clint Adams, Doc Matthews, and the desk clerk of the hotel, Avery, playing poker.

"Maybe they just wanna," Black said.

"What?"

"Maybe they just wanna play."

York scowled. He'd been told to leave Adams alone, but here were Doc and Avery playing poker with him, and Mike Black watching.

"Why are you here, Mike?" he asked.

"I'm watchin'—"

"I know you're watchin'," York said, "but why?"

Black hesitated, wondering if he was supposed to tell the sheriff anything.

"Mike?"

"The mayor."

"Mayor Biggers told you to watch Clint Adams?"

Black nodded.

"Why?"

"I don't know," Black said. "He just asked me to. You know, like for the good of the town?"

"Look," York said, "you go and watch the hotel from someplace else, okay?"

"Sure," Black said. "I was across the street, anyway. I just came over 'cause I was curious."

"Then go back across the street."

"Sure."

Black turned and left, and Sheriff York looked back into the room.

From across the street Mike Black was surprised to see, several minutes later, the mayor himself go into the hotel. He wondered if he was going to see Clint Adams, and if so, what was Sheriff York going to think of that?

Once Black left, Sheriff York was able to hear some of the conversation in the room, which consisted mostly of poker talk. Bet, raise, fold, deal. Then there was a knock at the door and Clint Adams called out, "Come in."

York was surprised to see Mayor Ed Biggers come through the door.

• • •

Clint didn't recognize the man who entered the room, but both Avery and Doc Matthews did.

"Mayor Biggers," Avery said.

"Hello, Ed," Doc said. "What brings you here?"

"Just thought I'd come by and say hello to our guest, Doc," Mayor Biggers said.

Clint was staring at Biggers. He couldn't help thinking how right Doc had been. The man was incredibly homely. It was difficult to imagine him with Mildred Haskell—or any woman, for that matter.

He was well-dressed, though, Clint had to give him that. Living in a small town did not seem to keep him from wearing good suits.

"Mr. Adams? I'm Mayor Ed Biggers. Please don't try to get up."

Clint wasn't going to try. Biggers extended his hand and Clint shook it.

"Would you like to play some poker, Mayor?" Clint asked.

"I'm afraid not," Biggers said. "I'm afraid I'm not much of a gambler."

"Not with cards," Doc said under his breath.

"How has Tucumcari been treating you, Mr. Adams?" Biggers asked, like a concerned host.

"Everyone's been real nice, Mayor," Clint said. "The people at the hotel here, even your secretary, Miss Haskell. I'm very impressed by her."

"Yes, Mildred is quite a gal," Biggers said. "I could never get along without her."

"You're a lucky man to have her, Mayor."

"I keep telling myself that," Biggers said. "I'm really

sorry this had to happen to you in our little town, Mr. Adams.''

''That's okay, Mayor,'' Clint said. ''I don't hold you responsible.''

''That's good. I hope once you're back up on your, uh, both feet, you'll stay around and let us show you some real hospitality.''

''Well, I understand you're having a party, of sorts.''

''Oh, yes,'' Biggers said, ''our Founder's Day. Yes, I suppose you could call it a big party of, uh, sorts.''

''That's what I've been hearing.''

Biggers looked at Doc and Avery, both of whom were watching him, and he realized that he could not talk to Adams here with them around. Also, he could have sworn he saw Sheriff Caleb York peeking in the window.

''Well, I see you're pretty busy,'' he said to Clint.

''Yeah,'' Clint said, ''we've got a pretty heavy game going here.''

''I just wanted to, uh, stop in and, uh, say hello and see if you needed, um, anything.''

''No,'' Clint said, ''I don't need a thing, Mayor, but thanks for asking.''

''Sure,'' Biggers said. ''We'll talk again before you leave town.''

''I'm sure we will.''

Biggers shook hands with Clint again and left.

''What was that all about?'' Avery asked.

''I'm sure I don't know,'' Doc said.

''He sure left in a hurry.''

''Maybe it has something to do with the sheriff peering in the window,'' Clint said.

''I wondered if you saw him,'' Doc said.

Avery, who had been sitting with his back to the window, turned quickly and said, "Where?"

Mike Black watched as the mayor came charging out of the hotel and went right into the alley next to it. Good. Now Sheriff York would get some of his own medicine.

TWENTY-FIVE

"What the hell are you doing here?" Biggers demanded, coming up behind York.

The sheriff turned, startled, and was struck dumb for the moment.

Biggers grabbed him by the arm and said, "Let's get out of here," and virtually pulled him from the alley.

Out in front of the hotel Biggers again demanded, "What are you doing?"

"I, uh, saw somebody in the alley and went to investigate."

"And who was it?"

"Mike Black."

"Black is across the street."

"I know," York said, "I made him leave the alley."

"So you could stay and watch?"

"I saw the other people in the room and was trying to find out what was going on."

"Why? I thought Mildred told you to stay away from Adams after your first talk."

"I'm still the sheriff here—"

"And that can be changed!" Biggers snapped, cutting

him off. "If you want to do your job, Sheriff, do it somewhere else."

"What about Black—"

"Mike Black is doing what I told him to do," Biggers said. "I suggest you do the same thing."

York glared at Biggers for a few seconds, then turned and walked away. Biggers watched, then went across the street to yell at Mike Black, as well.

Clint and Doc carried Avery for most of the evening, making sure the younger man didn't lose all his chips the first day. Clint called a halt to the game because Doc was starting to look haggard and he knew the older man would not admit he was tired.

"You did well, Avery," Clint said as the young man was leaving, "but tomorrow be ready to get wiped out."

"Ha," Avery said, much more comfortable with Clint than he had been the past two days, "I'm just gettin' started."

Avery left and Doc stood up from the table.

"How's the leg?"

Clint looked down at it and said, "Not bad."

"Sitting for a long time helps."

"You know," Clint said, "if we could get a fourth player we'd have a good game going."

"I'll look for one," Doc said. "I have to thank you for taking it easy on us, Clint. I know you could have wiped us out two or three times already."

"Don't be so sure," Clint said. "Like I said, the game is coming back to you."

Doc patted Clint on the arm and said, "I'll see you tomorrow, after lunch."

"We'll have to call the game early tomorrow."

"Why's that?"

"I'm having dinner with someone."

Doc's eyebrows went up.

"Mildred?"

Clint nodded.

"In here?"

Clint nodded again.

"Be careful of the leg," Doc said.

"I will."

Doc walked to the door.

"Doc?"

"Yes?"

"You were surprised when Mayor Biggers showed up here today?"

"Yes, I was."

"Why?"

Doc shrugged.

"Did you think he'd keep using Mildred to try to get to me?"

"I did, yes."

"Do you think he knows she's having dinner with me tomorrow?"

Doc thought a moment, then said, "Maybe not."

"You were right about him."

"In what way?"

"He is a homely son of a bitch."

Doc laughed.

"Yes, he is. Good night, Clint."

"Good night, Doc."

After Matthews left, Clint used his chair to walk over to the bed and lay down on it. Doc had been right, of course. He could have won all their chips almost any time he wanted. He was ahead, although he didn't know

how much of Doc's bill he had won back. In the end he
intended to pay the bill, anyway.

He checked the location of his gun, folded his arms
across his chest, and fell asleep.

Mike Black's ears were still burning from the tongue-
lashing he'd received from Mayor Ed Biggers. The
mayor called him stupid and told him to stay the hell
away from Clint Adams. In fact, he told him that he
wasn't needed anymore.

Black sat in the saloon nursing a beer along with a
grudge, wondering who was going to feel stupid when
the Tucumcari Kid came riding into town.

Mildred had intended to go to the hotel from the office. In fact, she had gotten as far as Clint's door, but
she could hear the voices inside and decided not to
knock.

At home that night she stood in front of her mirror
and held different dresses up in front of her. It had been
a long time since she had been in a hotel room with a
man other than Ed Biggers for the purposes of—well,
for social purposes. She was surprised at how nervous
she was about it.

Clint Adams was a very attractive and interesting man,
and she had no doubt that they were going to end up in
bed. What she didn't know was whether or not she
should tell Biggers about any of it.

After all these years, she wasn't sure if he would even
care, and that made her sad.

TWENTY-SIX

Clint woke the next morning and remained on the bed, going over some of what Doc had told him during their hours of poker. Of everything the older man had told him, he recalled the Tucumcari Kid. At the time the story of a young man who disliked his name had sounded funny, but thinking about it now Clint wondered about Harvey Little.

Over the years Clint had run across many young men who thought they were good with a gun. Some of them were, some weren't, but very few of them were as good as they thought they were. He had no idea how good this one thought he was, but suddenly he was sure that he was going to meet the young man. Someone who bore the name of the town was too good to be true for somebody like Ed Biggers, who was obviously ambitious. Clint suddenly knew that, one way or the other, he was going to have to cross paths with the Tucumcari Kid—and maybe Ed Biggers was counting on that.

He decided that he'd need to talk to the mayor again, and this time alone, just the two of them, and put all their cards on the table.

Just what would Ed Biggers do or *not* do to get his town on the map?

His opportunity to ask that question came sooner than he thought. Mildred came to his room with his lunch, as she had the day before, and asked if she could sit.

"Go ahead," he said. "I'll sit at the table with you. I want to ask you a question."

"Sure, go ahead."

"Tell me about the Tucumcari Kid."

She frowned, then laughed.

"Harvey Little? What about him?"

"That's what I'm asking you."

"What can I tell you about him?" she asked. "He's a local curiosity. He grew up here, didn't like his name, changed it and left."

"I hear he's good with a gun."

She looked uncomfortable.

"I wouldn't know about that."

"Does he have a reputation?"

"Around here, I guess he does, but nothing that you ever would have heard of. Why are you asking about him?"

"Doc mentioned something to me."

"Did he say he was good with a gun?"

"Very good."

"Then I guess he is," she said, standing up, leaning toward the door, "but he doesn't live here anymore."

"But does he still come around?"

"Sometimes, I guess. He hasn't been here for a while, though. Are you worried about having to face him, or something? I thought someone of your reputation didn't worry about that?"

"There's always somebody better," Clint said.

"Have you ever met anyone better than you?"

"If I had," he said, "I guess I wouldn't be here, but that just means he's out there someplace."

She looked at him with interest.

"Do you live with that every day?"

"I do."

"And you expect to meet him?"

"Who knows?" he said with a shrug. "Maybe I never will. Maybe he and I will never cross paths."

"I hope you don't," she said, "but I don't think you have to worry that it's Harvey Little."

"I thought nobody called him that anymore."

She made a face.

"The other name is just too silly. I have to get back to work. Do you still want me to come for dinner tonight?"

"Sure, why wouldn't I?"

"I thought maybe you and your poker buddies—"

"I'll shoo them away, don't worry," he said.

"About seven?"

"That'd be fine."

"That'll give me time to go home and change."

"I'll see you at seven, then."

She left and he remained at the table, finishing his sandwich. He thought if it wasn't for all the attention he'd been getting he would have gone crazy by now, but what was all this attention going to cost him?

Surely he'd be here by the time the Founder's Day festivities came along. Maybe he'd even be able to walk outside and watch, but he still had no intentions of playing any important role in their little party.

What were Mayor Biggers's plans for that day? he wondered.

Mike Black was back in his space across the street. He wasn't actually there to watch the hotel—although he could certainly see it. No, today he was waiting to see if the Kid was going to come riding in. When he did, he wanted to be able to tell him where Clint Adams was.

He wondered if the Kid would go for Adams right away or wait. Didn't he have an advantage now that Adams was laid up with a broken leg? Wouldn't he take that advantage? Or would he want to face Adams in the street, all fair and square?

Black didn't know what the Kid would do. He was probably one of the Kid's few friends, but he still couldn't ever predict what he would do.

That was for the Kid to know and for everyone else to find out.

TWENTY-SEVEN

When Doc and Avery showed up for the poker game Clint told them that they would have to break it up early that evening.

"But why?" Avery complained.

"Clint's got somethin' better to do with his time tonight," Doc said.

"Like what?"

"Never you mind," Doc said. "When he tells us to leave it's time to leave, with no questions. Understand?"

"No."

"That don't matter," Doc said. "Just shuffle and deal, lad. You might lose all your chips before then, anyhow."

Mike Black recognized him right off. He was still way down the street, but Black knew the way he sat a horse. Besides, the Kid had gotten himself the biggest horse he could find—it stood almost seventeen hands—and that made his five-foot-four frame sitting on that horse very distinctive.

Black stepped into the street to meet the Kid, and just stood there until the Kid reached him.

"Mike," the Tucumcari Kid said, nodding.

"Hello, Kid. I knew you'd come."

"Course you knew I'd come, you fool," the Kid said, "I sent you a telegram tellin' you I was comin'."

"Well, yeah, but I mean, before that. I knew you'd come before that."

"Never mind what you knew," the Kid said. "What you know wouldn't fill a pea, anyway. Where's Adams?"

"He's at the hotel, a ground-floor room."

"He alone?"

"He's got Doc and Avery with him."

"Who's Avery?"

"The desk clerk."

"What are they doin'?"

"They're playin' poker."

The Kid narrowed his eyes.

"I hear tell the Gunsmith is a pretty good poker player. What's he doin' playin' with them?"

"He's passin' the time, I guess. Can't go nowheres with his leg all broke."

"I suppose not."

"You gonna go in there and kill him?"

"Kill a man who's laid up with a broken leg? What kind of a reputation would that give me, Mike?"

"Then when you gonna do it?"

"When he heals," the Kid said. "When he's up and walkin' around and we can do it fair and square in the street."

"You're gonna face him in the street?"

"Well, sure."

"But . . . he's real good."

"So am I, Mike, you know that. Look, take my horse to the livery."

The Kid dismounted and handed Black the horse's reins.

"What are you gonna do?"

"I'm gonna get a hotel room."

"In the hotel?"

"Where else would I get a hotel room?"

"But . . . in the same hotel?"

"How many hotels are there in Tucumcari, Mike?" the Kid asked.

"Well, I just thought—"

"Don't think, Mike," the Kid said. "Just take care of my horse."

"What are you gonna do after you get a room?"

"I guess I'll get a drink."

"I'll meet you at the saloon, then."

"Fine, Mike," the Kid said. "I'll meet you there."

"We got lots to talk about, Kid."

"We'll see, Mike," the Kid said, not wanting to spend too much time actually *talking* with Mike Black, "we'll see. Okay?"

TWENTY-EIGHT

The word spread through town that the Kid was back, and eventually worked its way to Mayor Ed Biggers. Actually, Mildred heard it, and she told Biggers.

"Where is he?" Biggers asked, standing up and grabbing his hat.

"At the saloon, with Mike Black."

"I'm going over there."

"What are you going to tell him?" Mildred asked.

"Why, I'm just going to welcome him home," Biggers said as he went out the door.

When Biggers entered the saloon the Kid saw him, because he was sitting with his back to the wall.

"Well, well," he said to Black, "it's Hizzoner."

"What?" Black turned and saw Biggers approaching. "He yelled at me—" he started to say, but the Kid cut him off.

"He probably had a good reason."

"But—"

"Shut up."

Mayor Biggers reached them and put a big smile on his face.

"Kid," he said, "it's good to see you."

"Mayor Ed."

This was funny. The Kid had called Biggers "Mayor Ed" for years as a child, and continued to do so even when he changed his name to the Tucumcari Kid.

"Have a seat," the Kid said. "Mike, take a walk."

"Hey—"

"Mike!"

Feeling hurt, Black stood up and walked to the bar, carrying his beer.

"Want a beer, Mayor Ed?" the Kid asked as Biggers sat down.

"No, thanks, Kid."

"What'd you come over here for?"

"I heard you were in town," the mayor said. "I just wanted to welcome you back."

"Uh-huh," the Kid said. "How are things going for your Founder's Day celebration?"

"Oh, swell. Will you be here for that?"

"Well, gee, I don't know, Mayor," the Kid said. "I guess that would depend on when I conclude my business."

"Business? You're here on business?"

The Kid stared at Biggers until the older man began to fidget.

"Are we gonna play games, Mayor Ed? I thought we knew each other too well for that."

"What do you mean, Kid?"

"I mean Mike Black never would have sent me a telegram about Clint Adams being here unless you put him up to it."

"I never did," the mayor said. "You can ask Mike—"

"Oh, Mike wouldn't even know you did it," the Kid said. "He's not that smart. You're the one who wanted me to know the Gunsmith was here. You knew I'd be interested."

"So the Gunsmith is your business?"

"That's right."

"He's over at the hotel with a broken leg," the mayor said.

"I know, and he's playin' poker."

"A silly game, to pass the time," the mayor said. "You wouldn't be interested." Biggers knew that the Kid liked to play poker.

"You know what?"

"What?"

"I want to play in that game."

"What?"

"I want to play poker."

Biggers looked bewildered.

"But . . . why?"

"It'll give me time to study him," the Kid said, "and get to know him."

"But won't it give him time to get to know you?" Biggers asked.

"It'll give him time to sit across the table from me and wonder," the Kid said. "I'll be playin' with his head, Mayor Ed. You know all about doin' that, don't you?"

"Well—"

"Sure you do."

"So how are you going to get into the game?"

"I have a room at the hotel, on the second floor," the Kid said. "I guess I could knock on the door and say I heard about it, but I got a better idea than that."

"What?"

The Kid smiled.

"You're gonna get me into the game."

"Me? How?"

"Hey," the Kid said, "you're the mayor, figure out a way."

"Look, Kid—"

"Don't tell me you haven't talked to Adams yourself yet?" the Kid asked. "Have you been letting Mildred talk to him?"

"I've spoken to him."

"Then just go to his room and tell him that you have another player for him. He'll like that. A poker game is always better with four rather than with three."

"Kid—"

"Just do it, Mayor Ed," the Kid said harshly. "Do it!"

The mayor sat silently for a few moments, then said, "I'll try."

Inside, however, he was triumphant. The Kid was right, he did know how to play with people's minds.

TWENTY-NINE

Clint looked up when someone knocked on the door. "Come in."

Mayor Ed Biggers entered the room, drawing the attention of the three players.

"Hello, Mayor," Doc said.

"Doc," Biggers said. "Uh, Mr. Adams, I wonder if you'd be, uh, interested in a fourth player for your game?"

"Always glad to have a fourth player, Mayor," Clint said. "Pull up chair. I have to warn you, though, we're quitting early tonight."

"Well, no, it's not me," Biggers said, "and this person wouldn't start playing until tomorrow. He just got into town a while ago and he wants to rest."

"You tell your friend to come on by tomorrow afternoon, Mayor, and we'll have an empty chair waiting for him."

"Uh, okay, I'll tell him. Thank you."

"Thank *you*," Clint said. "I'm looking for a little more competition than these two have been giving me."

"Ha!" Doc said. "I've just been toying with you. Now I'm ready to play."

"Uh, me, too," Avery said nervously, but he wanted to be in on the banter.

"Well, all right," Biggers said. "I'll tell him."

He started to leave.

"Hey, Ed!" Doc said.

"Yes?"

"You didn't tell us who the new player is. Anybody we know?"

"Somebody you know, Doc," Biggers said, "but Mr. Adams, here, doesn't know him."

"What's his name?"

"Well," Biggers said, "it's not really a name as much as it's something he calls himself."

"He doesn't have a name?" Clint asked.

"Well, he does, but he doesn't like it very much, so he doesn't use it."

Doc and Clint exchanged a glance, both getting the same idea.

"Why do I get a bad feeling about this?" Doc asked.

"Who is it, Mayor?"

"Well, uh . . ."

"It's the Kid, isn't it, Ed?" Doc asked. "The Tucumcari Kid's in town."

"Well, yeah . . ."

"Are you crazy?" Doc asked. "You want to put the Kid in this room with Clint? You know what will happen."

"We'll play poker," Clint said, "that's what'll happen, Doc." He looked at Biggers. "You tell the Kid he's welcome in the game, Mayor."

"Uh, well, sure," Biggers said, surprised, "sure, Mr. Adams, I'll tell him."

As the mayor left, Doc looked across the table at Clint, baffled.

"What are you playin' at?" he asked. "I told you about him—"

"Doc," Clint said, "if the Kid is sitting at this table with us, he'll be right in front of me the whole time."

"You want to be able to keep an eye on him."

"Right."

"Still," Doc said, "bein' in the same room—"

"Is there gonna be shootin'?" Avery asked fearfully. "Uh, I can't play if there's gonna be shootin'."

Clint put his hand on Avery's arm and said, "Don't worry, Avery. There's not going to be any shooting."

Avery didn't looked appeased.

"Well," Doc said, "maybe not in the hotel."

As Ed Biggers left the hotel he was rubbing his hands together. This was going to work out even better than he'd planned. Yes, sir, much better than he planned.

THIRTY

Late in the afternoon Clint called a halt to the game.

"Have a good time," Doc said as he was leaving the room.

"Avery, don't leave yet," Clint said.

"Yes, sir?"

"I need to take a bath."

Avery frowned.

"Don't got no bathtubs in the hotel, Clint, and you can't leave the room—"

"Can you bring me something?"

"Like what?"

"Something bigger than a basin but smaller than a bathtub. I can just wash real good in it." Clint almost said he could take a "whore's bath," but he didn't think Avery would know what that meant.

"And I need some washcloths and towels."

Avery frowned even more, obviously giving the matter some thought.

"When do you need it by?"

"Within the hour?"

"I'll see what I can do, Clint."

"I'll pay you very well for success, Avery," Clint said. "That's a promise."

"That's okay, Clint," the younger man said. "I just wanna help. I'll see what I can do."

"Fine, thanks."

Avery left and Clint turned and looked around the room. He knew he needed a bath because he knew what was going to happen tonight between him and Mildred. He hoped Avery would be able to help him.

About twenty minutes had passed before there was a knock at the door for possibly the hundredth time in the past couple of days.

"Come," Clint said.

A triumphant Avery entered carrying an empty small metal tub.

"My mother uses it to do the laundry," he said, putting it down on the floor. It was larger than a bucket but smaller than a bathtub, just as Clint had asked.

"It's perfect, Avery. Thanks."

"I'll get the cloths and towels and soap, and then I'll bring up the water."

By six-thirty, Clint was washed, his hair was combed, he had fresh clothes on, and Avery had even managed to scare up a bottle of bay rum, which Clint used, but sparingly.

The food arrived before Mildred, which she had arranged in advance. Two waiters came into the room carrying a tray of food, a decanter of wine, and a pot of coffee—and a candle. They were leaving when she arrived.

"Enjoy it, ma'am," one of them said.

"We will," she assured them.

When she entered the room Clint admired her. Her dress was cut low to reveal the tops of her firm breasts, and her flesh was flawless. Her hair had been piled atop her head, revealing a long, graceful neck.

"You look beautiful."

She had worked on herself all day, attempting to recapture the absolute beauty of her youth.

"Thank you."

They sat down and started on their dinner, which consisted of steak and vegetables. They ate by candlelight and talked.

She told him how she had been born there when Tucumcari was just a few buildings and how she admired all of Mayor Biggers's efforts to get the town on the map.

"Just how far will he go to achieve that, Mildred?" he asked at one point.

She paused to think a moment, the glass of wine dangling from her hand.

"I think he'd do almost anything," she finally said.

"Almost?" he asked. "What wouldn't he do?"

She thought again, and then looked surprised.

"Now that you mention it, Clint," she said then, "I don't know what he wouldn't do."

"Murder?"

She frowned.

"That's a harsh word," he said then, taking her off the hook—almost. "Would he kill for it?"

"I . . . don't think he would actually kill, not in person."

"Then he'd hire it done?"

"This is hypothetical?"

"Yes."

"If it was the only way he could get it done, after all these years, then he probably would."

"And how do you feel about that?"

She shrugged.

"How should I feel? He's been at it a long time, Clint. What if there was something you wanted very badly for years, and year after year you just couldn't get it. Then, suddenly, it's within your grasp and all you have to do is have one person killed . . . would you do it?"

"No."

She looked surprised.

"Wouldn't it depend on who the person was?"

"No."

"A stranger?"

"No."

"A criminal?"

"No."

"An enemy?"

"No."

"No one?"

"No one," he said. "I wouldn't kill anyone for personal satisfaction or gain."

She sat back in her chair, ignoring the half of her dinner that was still remaining on her plate.

"But you have a reputation . . . for killing."

"I've only ever killed to protect myself or someone else. Never for any kind of personal gain."

"I find that hard to believe. I mean, I'm sorry, but in order to get a reputation like the one you have you must have had to kill a lot of people."

Clint toyed with his wineglass, turning it around and around. He was annoyed because this woman he found himself liking was questioning him in favor of his over-blown reputation.

"It's been my experience, Mildred, that reputations are usually less than half true," he said finally. "Take your Tucumcari Kid, for instance. He's all of twenty-five years old, as I understand it, and yet he's claiming to have killed more men than others twice his age. Do you think that's accurate?"

"No, I don't," she said, "but then I've known Harvey Little for a long time."

"Can you get away with calling him that?" he asked.

"What's he going to do?" she asked. "Shoot me?"

THIRTY-ONE

Mildred cleared the table of the plates and utensils and glasses, putting them on the dresser top, and they sat there and drank coffee, working their way up to... what? Clint wasn't even sure what was going to happen now that they'd had what might be called a difference of opinion.

"I didn't mean to offend you," she finally said.

"It's all right," he said. "Most people don't understand how out of proportion reputations can be."

"Well, I didn't," she said, "but you have to understand that all we see here in Tucumcari is what's in our newspaper, and that only comes out twice a month."

"Twice a *month*?"

She nodded.

"It used to come out once a month, so already we're twice as informed as we used to be."

They laughed about that, and they could both feel some of the tension beginning to drain away.

"That would be the *Tucumcari Courier*."

"Yes."

"I remembered."

"They'll be writing about Founder's Day for weeks," she said.

"Isn't it a big thing?"

She sighed.

"Ed—the mayor—wants it to be, but there aren't too many people in town who believe that."

"How many people *are* there in town, Mildred?"

"I don't know if we've got a hundred, Clint."

"Mildred, I understand about your loyalty to your home, and even to Mayor Biggers, but what about your loyalty to yourself?"

"Myself?"

"Yes. You should have a good life."

"I do."

"You're satisfied with the way your life is going?" he asked.

She frowned.

"I guess I don't think about my life much," she said. "I just live it, day to day."

"I think you deserve more than that," he said. "You're obviously very intelligent, and you sound educated."

"There's a school—there *was* a school—in the next county that my parents sent me to. Also, I read as much as I can, whenever I can get my hands on books or other newspapers, or even catalogues."

"So you sound largely self-educated."

"I don't know about that," she said. "You've probably known a lot of women smarter and more educated than I am."

"I think you could hold your own with any of the women I've ever met."

"Really?" She couldn't hide the fact that she was pleased.

"You're certainly as beautiful as any woman I've ever known."

"Well . . ."

"You are," Clint said, "you know you are. . . ."

"I know I was, at one time," she said, "but that was long ago. *That* was when I should have left, if I was going to leave, if I was going to accomplish something."

Clint got up and moved around to her side of the table. He felt clumsy, putting most of his weight on his left foot. He grabbed her by the arms and pulled her to her feet.

"Are you under the impression that you're too old to leave here and make a life somewhere else?"

She didn't answer, just stared at him.

"Mildred—"

She kissed him then, surprising not only him but herself. While they had both expected to have sex, the kiss was rather abrupt.

She had two reasons for kissing him. One was that she wanted to, and had wanted to for some time. The second was to shut him up, because he was starting to ask her questions she just didn't want to answer, questions about herself, and her perception of herself.

She'd rather just have sex and not think about anything else.

THIRTY-TWO

In a tight clinch they moved to the bed. She was kissing him like she hadn't kissed a man in a long time. He kissed her back the same way, because he liked the way she tasted.

They undressed each other hastily, laughing as they almost fell a couple of times because of his leg.

"Wait, wait, wait . . ." she finally said. She pushed him down onto the bed, where he sat with his pants around his ankles. "Just sit there."

He did as he was told and watched her finish undressing. When she was naked he was surprised at the size of her breasts. They were very full, with heavy undersides and large nipples.

"You're beautiful."

She looked away, then got on her knees and eased his trousers off very gingerly, so as not to hurt his leg. She tossed them away, then looked at him. His penis was rigid, jutting up from between his thighs. He thought he heard her make a sound like "umm" and then she ducked her head and took him fully into her mouth.

He put his hands palms down on the bed on either side of him, pressing down as she sucked him, moving his hips in time with her rhythm. After a few moments of that he took her head in his hands, letting her hair down and wrapping it around his fingers.

She made a very distinct sound of pleasure, like "Mmmmmm," and continued to suck him.

"Geez, Mildred—" he said.

She released him from her mouth and looked up at him, smiling. With her hair down and her mouth slack and soft, she looked incredibly beautiful. His penis was throbbing almost painfully, as if it was begging for release.

She stood up and straddled him. He took her buttocks in his hands as she lowered herself onto him. The head of his penis poked once, then pierced her. She was so wet, and when she sat down on him he went up deep inside of her, so deep that she gasped and he thought her eyes were going to roll up into her head. Sitting that way her feet were off the floor and her weight was on him.

"Oh," she said suddenly, "your leg."

"Don't you move," he said, even though his leg was killing him.

He lifted her, his hands still on her buttocks, taking her weight off his legs and totally into his hands. Her butt cheeks were slick with her wetness as he moved her up and down on him. She surrendered to him, let him control the pace. Her breasts were flattened against his chest, her arms were around him, and her lips were on his neck. He was again surprised that, aside from her breasts, she felt very slim, fragile even.

She was so light in his hands that he continued to increase the tempo, bouncing her up and down on him faster and faster until they were both grunting with the effort. Finally he felt her tremble and tense, and he exploded into her just as she started to scream and then stifled it by biting him on the shoulder.

He yelled. . . .

"I'm sorry," she said later, rubbing her hand over the bite.

"It's okay," he said. "I have other scars."

"Bites?"

He laughed.

"Bullets, knives . . . this will be my first bite scar."

She snuggled up against Clint, sighing contentedly. Sex with him had made her times with Biggers, and the sheriff, and other men seem ridiculous. When he left she didn't know how she was going to be able to stay with Ed Biggers. The best thing for her to do would be to leave Ed to his wife and find another place to live, another town.

But before she left, she had to decide where her loyalties really were, with Ed Biggers, a man she had known all her life, or with Clint Adams, the best lover she had ever been with, but a man she had known only two days.

It would be a tough choice.

THIRTY-THREE

The Tucumcari Kid sat in his room smoking a cigarette and thinking about Clint Adams. When he was alone he couldn't help but think of himself as Harvey Little, even though he had given up that name long ago. He knew he was the Kid, but he had been born Harvey and it was hard to simply disremember a name you were born with.

To the world outside he was the Kid, a young man who had killed forty, fifty, a hundred men, depending on who you believed.

In his room, he knew that he had killed three men in fair fights. The Kid knew he was good with a gun. He knew he could hit anything he pointed a pistol at, and he knew he could get his gun out of his holster real quick, but none of the men he had killed had been a real test for him.

Now he had the chance to really test himself, against a man who was as famous as Hickok, Earp, and Masterson. He knew he'd be taking a big chance. He knew that Clint Adams might kill him. But he also knew if he killed Adams, then he'd be as famous as Hickok, Earp, Masterson, *and* the Gunsmith.

That might not have been worth the risk for a lot of men, but it was worth it for the Tucumcari Kid.

It was also worth it for Harvey Little.

THIRTY-FOUR

Mildred stayed the whole night and they made love twice more, once when she woke him, and again when he woke her. Clint found the longer she stayed, the less he noticed the pain in his leg.

In the morning they slept late, having tired each other out. Also, since his window looked out on the alley the sun did not stream into the room and wake them.

"I can bring some breakfast back," she said as they dressed.

Avery had conveniently forgotten to bring the coffee at nine a.m.

"Just have Avery bring the coffee," he said. "You probably have to go to work."

"Yes, I do."

She was hesitant to leave the room, though, and he knew she was trying to decide if she should tell him something. Judging by the amount of trouble she was having, it was probably something that would make her feel disloyal.

"Mildred?"

"Hmm?"

120

"Is there something on your mind?"

She looked away.

"There's been something on my mind since I first met you," she said.

"I thought we took care of that last night."

She smiled then and looked at him.

"Yes, we did."

"There's something else, though."

"Yes."

"Something you think I should know?"

"Yes."

"But you're not sure yet that you can tell me."

"Right."

"Well, then, wait."

"What?"

"Wait," he said. "Don't tell me anything until you're very sure you want to."

"How can you say that?" she asked. "It might be something very important."

"All the more reason you should wait, then. There's time, isn't there?"

"Yes," she said quietly, "there's time."

"Get out of here, then," he said. "Go to work and I'll see you later."

"When?"

"Whenever you're ready," he said. "I'm not going anywhere."

She leaned over and kissed him on the mouth softly.

"You're an unusual man."

"That's only because you're judging me by the men you've met in this one town. Wait until you've traveled and met more."

"It won't matter," she said. "You'll still be an unusual man."

As she was going out the door, he yelled, "And don't forget to send Avery up with the coffee!"

THIRTY-FIVE

Ed Biggers woke up and looked at his wife, lying next to him. They'd had sex the night before, the first time in weeks. Usually, when Biggers got the urge—not so often, lately—he had Mildred take care of it, but lately Mildred didn't seem to be enjoying that part of their relationship. He'd come home last night and, for some reason, had felt like having sex. He'd looked across the table at his wife, who usually did not arouse him, and suddenly his penis was raging.

Ethel was surprised when he came around the table and pulled her to her feet, even more surprised when he raised her nightgown to paw her breasts. She had never been a pretty woman, but she had firm, almost chubby breasts, and he'd forgotten how pretty her nipples were. They were pinkish, while Mildred's were dark brown. When he leaned over and took one breast in his mouth, she had gasped and said, "Eddie!"

She hadn't called him that in years. For some reason, it aroused him even more.

He ended up taking her in the kitchen, bending her over the table, raising her nightgown to reveal her ass, and then sliding into her from behind. She was wet right away, and for a moment he considered withdrawing from her vagina and putting it in her ass, but he decided not to. It was something he had only done with Mildred, and he was surprised he had even gotten this far with Ethel. They'd never had sex in the kitchen before.

She grunted and moaned while he fucked her like that, and at one point he thought the table would give way beneath them. Finally, with a loud roar, he exploded into her, and she screamed as he had never heard her scream before.

Now he looked down at her lying next to him, naked. They had gone to bed and made love again, only it wasn't making love, it was just having sex. He had pulled her atop him the second time, so he could suck on her breasts while she rode him. He knew Ethel must have been wondering what had gotten into him, but she never complained, not even when he pushed her down between his legs so she could take him in her mouth. They had argued about this before, but on this night it seemed as if anything and everything was all right— although he still did not try to put it in her ass. He thought that she'd balk at that and ruin the mood.

She was lying on her back, and her chubby breasts did not look as chubby or as pretty this morning. They were sort of flopped to either side of her as she lay on her back. Also, in repose, her homely face became even more homely, and he could not imagine that he had been in her mouth last night. He eased himself from the bed, not wanting to wake her for fear that she would want to have sex again.

He must have wanted it *real* bad last night.

• • •

Sheriff Caleb York woke the next morning, feeling dissatisfied with himself. He was still the sheriff, still the law in Tucumcari, and today he wanted to act like it.

He knew that the Tucumcari Kid had come into town yesterday, and while he had been told to stay away from Clint Adams, no one had said anything about the Kid.

He left his office—he had slept on a cot in one of the cells—and started for the hotel. He thought he might as well have breakfast there, too.

The Tucumcari Kid woke the next morning with the sun shining through the window into his eyes. He rolled over to get away from it, then sat up and looked around. He was ravenously hungry, so he dressed quickly and went downstairs to have breakfast.

He was seated at a table with a breakfast of steak and eggs in front of him when the sheriff entered the dining room. He chewed his food slowly, watching as the man crossed the room to him.

"Morning, Kid."

"Sheriff," the Kid said with a nod. "What can I do for you?"

"Just wanted to stop by and say hello."

York started to sit, but the Kid stopped him.

"I didn't invite you to sit with me."

York stopped short, then looked around to see if anyone had heard the Kid talk to him like that.

"Take it easy, Kid—"

"If you want to say something to me, say it and then leave me alone," the Kid said. "If you want to have breakfast, sit at another table and eat it. I eat alone."

"Kid," York said, "I just wanted to—"

"You wanted to act like a sheriff today and come

across to bother me during my breakfast and ask me
what I was doing in town.''

''I just—''

''You'll find out what I'm doing here when everybody
else does, Sheriff. Is there anything else?''

''Uh, n-no—''

''Then I'll finish my breakfast in peace . . . if you
don't mind.''

''N-no, Kid, I don't mind. . . .''

The Kid had already gone back to his meal and forgotten about York.

Having lost his appetite the sheriff left the dining
room, and the hotel, and went back across the street to
his office, where he should have stayed.

THIRTY-SIX

The Kid decided not to rush his entry into the game. Biggers had told him the night before that the way had been cleared for him to play. Now that Adams was expecting him, the Kid decided to keep him waiting. He decided to take a chair out in front of the hotel and just sit for a while.

While he was there the doctor came to the hotel, undoubtedly to start the game that day.

"Hello, Kid."

"Doc."

"It's good to see you."

"You, too, Doc."

"I understand you're going to play some poker with us?" the doctor said.

"I thought I might join in, yeah. Is that all right with you, Doc?"

"Me? Oh, sure, it's fine with me, Kid. There's not a lot of money in the game, you know. We're just sort of passing the time."

"Until the Gunsmith's leg heals, right?"

"Uh, yes, that's right."

"How bad was the break?"

"More of a fracture, actually."

"How did it happen?"

"He got kicked by a horse in the livery."

"Ow," the Kid said sympathetically, "I'll bet that hurt."

"It did, indeed. Well, I'd better get inside. You comin'?"

"In a little while, Doc," the Kid said. "I'll be there in a little while."

"Uh, okay, fine," Doc said, "see you then."

The Kid touched the tip of his hat, and the doctor went inside.

The Kid settled back in his chair, satisfied with the way the day was going so far. Doc would tell Adams that he was sitting outside, in no apparent hurry to join the game. Let Adams wait and wonder when he would come by. Let him anticipate meeting the Tucumcari Kid.

When Doc Matthews entered the hotel, Avery came around the desk.

"Doc, he's outside," the desk clerk said urgently.

"I saw him, Avery."

"What are we gonna do?"

"Nothin'."

"Are you gonna tell Clint?"

"I'll tell him."

"What do you think he'll do?"

"I think he'll play poker, Avery," Doc said. "When are you comin' to the game?"

"Uh, I don't know if I can—"

"Don't be chicken, son," Doc said, putting his hand on the other man's shoulder. "If there's shootin' nobody will be shootin' at us, and it'll probably be somethin' you can tell your grandkids about.''

"I guess you're right," Avery said thoughtfully. "Uh, I get off the desk at one. I'll come in then."

"Fine."

"You think the Kid will be there by then?"

"I don't know."

Now it seemed as if the man was afraid he'd miss something.

"If you see him come in and head for Clint's room, why don't you just tag along?"

"I'll do that, Doc," Avery said. "I'll do that."

"See you later, son."

"Sure, Doc."

Avery went back around behind the desk, and Doc headed down the hall to Clint's room, which was only one of two that were on the ground floor. He didn't seriously think there'd be any shooting in the hotel, and probably none at all until Clint could stand, but he didn't see any chance in hell of a shooting being totally avoided.

Which probably made Mayor Ed Biggers extremely happy.

Ed Biggers was almost dressed and out of his bedroom when his wife woke up.

"Eddie?"

He cringed at the sound of the name that had so inflamed him the night before. He looked at the bed and she was sitting up, still naked. Her face was a mass of wrinkles, and this morning her breasts looked deflated. To make it even worse, she assumed a look she probably thought was playful, or sexy. Instead, she looked pained.

"Come back to bed, Eddie."

"I have to go to work, Ethel," he said. "I'll see you this evening."

"Mmmm," she said, stretching her arms above her head—not a pretty sight—"I'll be ready for you again tonight, Tiger."

Tiger! She had *never* called him that before.

"Don't wait up for dinner, Ethel," he said. "I may have to work late."

Her face fell, which was even more frightening than her sexy look.

"But, Ed—"

"There's lots to do, you know, in preparation for Founder's Day."

Biggers just about ran from the room, leaving his wife to puzzle over what had happened last night. Had it been a dream? No, she was still sore from him having sex with her twice, after not touching her for weeks. Also, his fluids were dry on her thighs, a definite sign that what had happened last night *had* really happened.

What she didn't know was why, and she really shouldn't have been surprised that, come morning, he was back to normal.

She lay back down in bed, staring at the ceiling, re-playing the scene from the kitchen. She supposed the memory of last night would have to sustain her for a few more weeks, at least.

THIRTY-SEVEN

When Doc entered Clint's room he immediately said, "The Kid is sitting out in front of the hotel."

Clint smiled. He was already seated at the table, having dealt himself a hand of solitaire.

"You find that funny?"

"He thinks he's making me wait."

"Isn't he?" Doc asked, sitting across from him.

"Well, yeah, but he thinks he's giving me time to think, and to worry."

"And are you worried?"

"No, Doc."

"And why not?"

"Because all we're going to do is play cards."

"Are you sure?"

"If he wanted to call me out he would have done it, by now."

"You can't stand."

"Which leads me to believe that he wants to wait until I can. Apparently, he's going to want it to be a fair fight. Does he have a reputation as a back-shooter, or a bushwhacker?"

"No," Doc said, "from everything I've heard, every man he's killed has had a fair chance."

"See? Just poker. Besides, there's something else that he hasn't figured out yet."

"And what's that?"

Clint collected the cards together and began to shuffle.

"He's making himself wait, as well."

When Avery joined the game at 1:15 the Kid had still not arrived.

"He's still sitting out there," Avery announced when he entered.

"Well," Clint said, "he can't win any money from out there. He'll be in soon enough. Take your seat, Avery. Doc needs you to change the luck of the cards."

Avery looked over at the rumpled bed as he sat down, and then at Clint, who winked at him.

"Was the coffee okay this morning?" the desk clerk asked.

"It was fine," Clint said, "but it was a bit late."

"Well," Avery said, "I just thought . . ." He looked embarrassed.

"You thought right, Avery," Clint said, completing his shuffle. "The cards are coming out, gentlemen. Jack for Avery, king for Doc, ace for me, looks like an interesting hand. . . ."

Out in front of the hotel the Tucumcari Kid was still sitting, as he had been for hours. At one point he saw Mildred Haskell across the street, walking toward the mayor's office. He hadn't seen her in a while, and he thought she was looking particularly pretty today, even if she was a little too old for him.

* * *

Mildred had stopped at home before going to work, to bathe and dress freshly. She saw the Kid sitting in front of the hotel on her way to work, and she told Biggers about it when she arrived at his office.

"What's he doing?" the mayor asked.

"Just sitting."

"That's all?"

"That's it."

"I'll have to talk to him," the mayor said, standing up. "You look different this morning."

"Do I?"

"Sort of . . . radiant."

"Thank you," she said, looking away.

"You did it, didn't you?"

"Did what?"

"You went to bed with him."

She didn't answer.

"It doesn't matter," Biggers said, "really. I mean, we're not married, are we?"

"No, we're not."

"Besides," he said on his way to the door, "I did it last night, too."

"Did what?"

"I had sex with Ethel."

That startled her.

"With Ethel?"

He nodded.

"I don't know what happened," he said. "One minute we were sitting in the kitchen and the next I've got her bent over the table—"

"Please," Mildred said, putting her hand over her mouth, "that's more than I want to know."

"And we did it again, later, in bed."

"How did Ethel take it?"

"She loved it," he said.

"And you?"

"When I woke up and looked at her . . ." he said, then shuddered and stopped. "I don't think I'll go home tonight. She might think we're going to do it again."

He left the office, shaking his head, and Mildred started to laugh as soon as the door closed behind him.

THIRTY-EIGHT

The Kid was about to go inside to join the game when he saw Mayor Biggers coming toward him. He decided to wait just long enough to give the mayor a hard time.

"Kid."

"Mayor."

"I, uh, thought you'd be playing poker."

"I'm going to."

"When?"

"In a little while. Were you worried I wouldn't get into the game?"

"No, no," Biggers said, "Adams said there'd be a chair for you, and I'm sure there will be." Biggers looked at his watch.

"Don't worry, Mayor," the Kid said. "I won't miss it."

"No, no," Biggers said, "I know you won't."

"Let me ask you something, Mayor."

"What's that, Kid?"

"Would you like me to wait until Founder's Day to kill Adams?"

"Uh, Founder's Day to, uh, kill him? In front of all those people?"

"You really think there'll be a lot of people, Mayor?" the Kid asked.

"Well, sure," Biggers said, "the whole town will be there."

The Kid laughed.

"Even if the whole town does show up, Mayor, there won't be a lot of people."

"What are you getting at, Kid?"

"You want me to kill Adams," the Kid said, "or Adams to kill me. Either way you'll get what you want, and that's some attention. Right?"

The mayor didn't answer. He looked away down the street, as if checking to see if someone was coming for him.

"You don't have to answer," the Kid said. "I know that's the case. How about if it happens before Founder's Day? Maybe people would turn out then from all over the county to see the winner. Hey, the winner could even cut your ribbon for you. I heard you were looking for somebody to do that. Did you ask Adams?"

"We did."

"And?"

"He turned us down."

"Uh-huh," the Kid said. "That means you'll be wanting me to win, won't you?"

Now Biggers looked right at the Kid.

"If you do win," he asked, "would you cut the ribbon, Kid?"

"Sure, Mayor," the Kid said, "I'll be your celebrity. That's what you want, right? A celebrity?"

"That's right."

"Well, then," the Kid said, "all I have to do is outdraw Clint Adams in front of witnesses, and that's what I'll be.''

''So,'' the mayor said, ''when will you do it?''

''As soon as Doc says he can walk out of this hotel and into the street.''

''Isn't that risky?'' the mayor asked. ''I mean, waiting for him to get all healed.''

''I suppose so,'' the Kid said, ''but it's the only way it'll do me any good. I don't want to be known as the man who bushwhacked the Gunsmith, or shot him because he couldn't stand. I want to be the man who outdrew him.''

''Fine,'' the mayor said, ''whatever you want.''

''I'll tell you what else I want.''

''What?''

''When I do it I want you to be there.''

''What?''

''I want you to be one of the witnesses.''

The mayor didn't answer.

''Or I'll ride out and forget the whole thing.''

''Okay,'' the mayor said, ''all right, I'll be there. Is there anything else?''

The Kid hesitated, then said, ''Your secretary.''

''Mildred? You want her to be there?''

''No,'' the Kid said, ''I want her to be in my bed afterward, naked and ready for me. Can you guarantee me that, Mayor?''

''If that's what you want, Kid.''

''That's what I want.''

''Isn't she a little old for you?'' Biggers asked. ''Wouldn't you like me to get you someone younger—''

''I want her,'' the Kid said, cutting him off. ''Sure,

she's older, but she's also experienced. She'll be able to teach me something, won't she?''

"Sure, Kid," Biggers said, "sure, whatever you want.''

"Well," the Kid said, standing up, "I guess I've kept the Gunsmith waiting long enough, haven't I? Time to go play some poker.''

"Good luck, Kid.''

"Thanks, Mayor," the Kid said, "it's right nice of you to want me to win at poker.''

Biggers nodded, and the Kid went into the hotel, thinking that playing games with Biggers's mind was getting to be a lot of fun.

The mayor headed back to his office, wondering how he was going to explain this to Mildred.

Maybe the Gunsmith would kill the Kid, and he wouldn't have to.

THIRTY-NINE

When Clint heard the knock at the door he knew it was the Kid. It was a totally different knock than what he had been hearing for the past few days. Most of the people who had knocked at his door were not sure they wanted to come in. This was a firm, I-want-to-come-in knock if he'd ever heard one.

"Come in."

There were no surprises when the Kid walked in. Clint had been told that he was short in stature and he was, and he'd been told he was young, and he looked it. He'd also been told that the Kid had killed men with his gun—the amount didn't matter, but he *had* killed, and Clint could tell from looking into the young man's eyes that this was true, as well.

Whether he called himself Harvey Little, or the Tucumcari Kid, this young man was a killer, of that there was little doubt.

"I understood there was a friendly poker game going on in here," he said easily.

"You came to the right place, friend," Clint said. "We just happen to have an empty chair—or were we saving that for somebody, Doc?"

"We were saving it for him, Clint," Doc said. "Clint Adams, meet the Tucumcari Kid."

The Kid sat down and made no move to shake hands.

"Pleased to meet you, Mr. Adams," he said. "I've heard a lot about you."

"I've been hearing about you this week, too, Kid. Do you mind if I call you Kid?"

"I prefer it," the Kid said. "But I'll bet what you heard about me is nothing like what I've heard about you, sir."

Sir, Clint thought, very respectful.

"What do you say we forget what we heard, Kid," Clint asked, "and just see what we can find out about each other, huh?"

"Sounds fair to me," the Kid said. "What's the name of the game?"

"Dealer's choice."

"What's the buy-in?"

"Oh, Doc'll give you some chips and we'll worry about who won what later. We're just passing the time here. I don't know if you heard, but I was fool enough to go and get kicked by a horse, and I've got a fractured leg."

"I did hear somethin' about that, I think," the Kid said, raking in the cards Clint had just dealt for a hand of five-card draw.

"What does a fella need to open in this game?" he asked.

"Guts," Clint said.

The Kid smiled and said, "I'll open," and tossed a white chip into the center of the table.

• • •

Three hours later Clint knew one thing. The Kid knew how to play poker—so well, in fact, that both Avery and Doc were out of the game.

"I'm busted," Avery said. "I thought this was supposed to be a friendly game?"

"I'm sorry," the Kid said, looking at Avery and Doc, "was I not supposed to win?"

"Hey," Doc said, "if you can win, you win. You earned all those chips."

"I don't have any more than what Clint has," the Kid said. During the first hour of the game he'd started calling Clint by his first name.

"I tell you what," he went on, "just to make it interesting, Clint, why don't you give Avery some of your chips, I'll give Doc some of mine, and we'll just keep on passin' the time. Whataya say?"

"Sounds good to me," Clint said, so that's what they did and the game continued.

Over the course of the next two hours the Kid's style of play had changed. It was as if he had already proven his point, and now he was just playing for fun. He didn't bluff any hands—he had bluffed Avery and Doc out twice—and he never raised more than a couple of chips, and never more than twice.

The game progressed slowly, but Clint and the Kid watched each other, and learned.

Before the game had started that day, Clint, mindful of the fact that the Kid was going to play, had removed his gun from the bedpost and had hung it on the back of his chair, so it was close at hand.

As soon as he entered the room the Kid noticed this,

and Clint *saw* that he noticed it. There was always the
chance that the Kid would come into the room with his
gun blazing, and Clint wanted to put himself in a position to defend himself if that happened. However, he had
not *expected* that to happen, and it had not. Still, he
wanted the Kid to know that he'd be ready for anything,
and that's what hanging his gun on the back of his chair
was meant to convey.

The Kid, of course, saw the gun as soon as he entered
and silently approved. In looking at the Gunsmith he saw
a man who was not particularly remarkable-looking to
him. He did not have the predatory look of a Doc Hol-
liday, or the refined look of a Bat Masterson, and the
Kid had seen both of those men. What the Kid did see
in Clint Adams was a relaxed, confident man with eyes
that had seen dead men. He knew that Clint Adams saw
in his eyes the same thing. They recognized each other
for what they were, and would have done so from across
a crowded room.

The Kid also saw a man who was confident in the
way he played cards. While he had been able to bluff
Avery and Doc with ease, he never once was able to
bluff Clint. He tried twice, and Clint not only called his
bet but raised it. It was as if the man could read his
mind, or as if his cards were see-through, and Clint could
see them.

He had to admit that Clint Adams was a better card
player than he was. The Kid thought if he lived ten more
years he might get as good as Clint, but there was a
chance he might not live past the next two weeks, if

Clint Adams was as good with a gun as he was with a deck of cards.

Of course, if he wasn't, then it was Clint Adams who had less than two weeks to live.

FORTY

Clint broke the game up early enough for Mildred to come to his room, if she wanted.

"Well," the Kid said, "that was a pleasant day's diversion. I thank you gentlemen for lettin' me sit in."

"We'll be playin' again tomorrow," Avery said enthusiastically. Then he looked at Clint and asked, "Won't we?"

"Yes, we will, Avery," Clint said. He looked at the Tucumcari Kid. "You're welcome to play again tomorrow, if you like, and every day after that for as long as you're here."

"How long is this game gonna go on?" the Kid asked.

"Oh, probably just until the Doc gives me the okay to walk around on this leg."

"Well, then, I'll be here tomorrow," the Kid said. "Thanks for the invite."

He turned to Avery and slapped the man on the back, startling him.

"Come, Avery, I'll walk you out."

"Uh, okay."

As they went out the door Clint heard the Kid say, "How about I buy you a drink?"

He didn't hear the clerk's reply.

Clint looked over at the table and saw Doc still sitting there.

"What's wrong, Doc?"

The old man looked up at him.

"I just thought I'd see what you thought of him," the physician said.

"The Kid? He strikes me as being very confident, without being cocky. He's also a fair to middling card player. Given a few more years, he'd be a good one."

"Does he have a few more years?"

"There's no way I can tell that, Doc," Clint said. "I'm not a fortune-teller."

"Will he have a few years left if he goes up against you?"

"Can't tell that either," Clint said. "I've seen him handle a deck of cards, but I haven't seen him handle a gun yet."

"Do you believe he's killed men with his gun?"

"Oh, yes."

"You can tell that by looking at him?"

"Yes."

"And he can tell it about you?"

"I'm sure he can."

Doc stood up.

"Where is it on a man that you can see that, Clint?" he asked, with real interest.

"In the eyes, Doc," Clint said. "It's all in the eyes."

FORTY-ONE

The Tucumcari Kid came back the next day to play, and the day after that, and the day after that. He played a lazy game, just sitting and not talking very much, then being gregarious after the game, inviting Doc and Avery to the saloon for a drink. He simply wanted to be in Clint's face as much as possible.

Mildred came back every night for the rest of the week, still wondering if she should tell Clint that Ed Biggers was planning to pit him against the Kid in an attempt to attract attention to the town. Every night, while lying in Clint's arms, she swore she would tell him, and by the light of day she felt that would be disloyal to Biggers.

Mayor Biggers spent the rest of the week trying to avoid his wife, keeping an eye on the hotel, hoping that there would not be any sudden eruptions of gunfire. He wanted the Gunsmith and the Kid to go at it on the street, where everyone could see what was happening.

* * *

Doc watched with interest as Clint and the Tucumcari Kid sat across from each other day in and day out, barely looking at one another, it seemed. Supposedly they were playing poker, but he knew there was another game going on beneath the surface, and that was the game that fascinated him.

He was also impressed with the Kid. He had not seen him in a very long time, and was surprised to find out that the young man had developed a sort of charm. He used that charm an Avery, convincing the desk clerk every night over a beer that they were friends.

Doc stopped and had a beer with them once or twice, but usually went straight home, too exhausted to do anything else.

Sometimes he found himself wishing one of them would shoot the other, so that the game would stop. He refused to quit, though. He'd keep playing as long as they did . . . and as long as he was still breathing.

Founder's Day was rapidly approaching. Signs were starting to appear around town, nailed up on the sides of buildings or displayed in store windows, and banners had been hung at both ends of town.

Both Mike Black and Sheriff Caleb York sulked at having been dismissed and/or yelled out and just generally left out of everything that was going on.

Black saw the Kid each night in the saloon with that desk clerk, and once or twice with Doc Matthews. Was the Kid getting real friendly with the poker players, including Clint Adams? If he got friendly with the Gunsmith, would he forget about his plan to kill him? He hoped not. If the Kid killed Adams, and became the man who killed the Gunsmith, then Mike Black's stature, as the Kid's friend, could only increase.

Then nobody would dare yell at him.

Founder's Day was three days away when Doc told Clint, "I think it's time you tried walking around a bit."

"You mean outside?"

Doc nodded. He hadn't closed the door behind him, and now he stepped back out into the hall and then came back in carrying a pair of crutches.

Clint made a face.

"Do I have to use those?"

Doc nodded.

"Both?"

"Both or one," Doc said, "your choice."

Clint took the two crutches and stood up. He tried it first with both, jamming them under his arms. He knew that a few hours of that would make his armpits sore. He then tried one and decided he could get around that way.

"What about this contraption you've got on my leg?" he asked.

"I want to leave the splint on longer," the doctor said, "just to be sure."

Clint moved around the room with the one crutch experimentally, trying first under one arm, then the other. He decided to use it on his injured side, which would keep the weight off that foot.

"Want to go for a walk?" Doc asked.

"I thought you'd never ask."

FORTY-TWO

There was a problem with his boots, so Clint waited while Doc went out and got a pair of boots that was a size or two bigger than his normal boot. Clint still didn't want to ruin a good pair of boots by cutting his.

When Doc returned he had a worn, secondhand pair of boots. Clint decided to wear his regular boot on his uninjured foot, using the one Doc brought for his fractured leg. When he stood up on them he announced that the fit was adequate.

"Let's go for a walk, then," Doc said.

He opened the door and let Clint leave ahead of him. Clint paused to first strap on his gun. There was no way he was going to leave his room without it. They walked down the hall at Clint's pace, which was slow and would be until he got used to using the crutch. For Clint, just being in the hall was an accomplishment.

When they got to the lobby Avery looked up from the desk.

"Hey, Clint," he called out. "You're up and around."

"Up and around," Clint said, "but not too spryly."

"Hey," the desk clerk said, "you got to start somewhere. Does this mean we ain't gonna play today?''

"We'll play when I get back, Avery."

Avery's expression became serious.

"You're going out?"

"Just for a short walk, to try out my leg."

"Do you, uh, think that's smart?"

"Doc says it's okay."

"We just won't stay out too long."

"But—"

Both Clint and Doc knew what Avery was referring to, but pretended that they didn't. Doc waved and he and Clint went out the front door.

Mike Blank instantly saw a way to get back into the good graces of somebody, either the Kid or the mayor. He saw Doc and Clint Adams come out the front door of the hotel and thought that someone should know that Adams was back on his feet.

But who?

When he made his decision, he waited for Doc and Clint Adams to commit to a direction. Once they started walking, he left his doorway and crossed the street.

"Let's go slowly," Doc reminded Clint. "I'm probably letting you up too early, as it is, I don't want to put too much pressure on that leg. It's my opinion that the fracture wasn't too bad. I don't want you to prove me wrong."

"I won't."

"Where do you want to go?"

Clint answered without hesitation.

"To the livery. I want to go and see Duke."

"Who?"

"My horse."

"Oh. Well, okay, let's go and see your horse, but, uh, do you, uh, really think you should be around horses again, so soon, after what happened last time?"

"Shut up."

When they reached the livery, Jake, the liveryman, came out to meet them.

"Looks like you're back on your feet," he said to Clint.

"One of them, anyway. How's my horse?"

"He's fine," Jake said. "Me and him came to a understandin'."

"What kind of understanding?"

"I feed him," Jake said, "and I never try to touch him."

"That sounds like Duke."

He left Doc outside with Jake and went in to see the big gelding.

"How you doin', fella?" he asked. He gave wide berth to the horse who had kicked him on the way to Duke's stall.

The big black gelding's head turned and he stared balefully at Clint.

"Bet you thought I left you, huh?"

He moved alongside the horse and touched his massive neck. If anyone else had done that they might have lost some fingers, but since Clint and Duke were partners the gelding suffered his touch.

Clint didn't overdo it. He patted the horse's neck, spoke to him for a few minutes, and then left him, satisfied that he had let Duke know that he was still around.

"Is he okay?" Doc asked.

"He's fine. Thanks for taking care of him, Jake."

"Sure thing."

"I think we should get back now," Doc said.

"Okay." Clint didn't argue, because already his arm-pit was getting sore from the crutch.

They left the livery and walked back to the hotel. As they approached they noticed somebody sitting out in front of it.

"Uh-oh," Doc said.

They both recognized the man at the same time.

"Just relax, Doc," Clint said. "No reason to get excited."

"We're outside now," Doc said, "not in your room at a poker table."

"Just relax," Clint said. "I'll take care of it."

They continued on, and as they approached the hotel the Tucumcari Kid stood up from his chair to await them.

FORTY-THREE

Clint and Doc stopped about ten feet from the Kid. Across the street Clint could see a man watching them. Doc recognized the man as Mike Black and immediately realized what had happened. Black had seen Clint out on his feet and had run immediately to the Kid.

"Nice to see you up and around, Clint," the Kid said. "Does this mean no game today?"

"There's a game," Doc said. "Clint's far from back on his feet. I just wanted him to test the leg a little."

"What do you say, Clint?" the Kid asked. "Got your balance back?"

"Not quite," Clint said. "I'm thrown off a bit by this crutch."

"And if you were to get rid of the crutch?"

Clint laughed.

"I'd probably fall down on my face."

Doc suddenly saw the Kid's entire demeanor change. He hadn't realized that the Kid had been so tense until he relaxed and his shoulders actually seemed to go down a few inches.

"So when's the game going to start?"

"About an hour," Doc said. "Clint's going to have to rest up from this little walk."

"That's okay," the Kid said, sitting himself back down. "I can wait."

Clint knew that the Kid wasn't talking about the poker game.

He and Doc walked past the Kid and into the lobby. They walked in silence to Clint's room, where he sat heavily on the bed, laying the crutch on the floor next to it. He took off his gun belt and hung it on the bedpost.

"That was close," Doc said. "I thought he was going to—"

"No," Clint said, "he wasn't."

"How could you tell?"

"Like I've told you before, Doc," Clint said, "it's all in the eyes."

"I guess I was watching the wrong part of his body," the doctor said.

"What was that?"

"His gun hand."

"His gun hand would be the third part of his body to know he was going to draw."

"The eyes would be first?"

"No," Clint said, "first the brain, and then the eyes would mirror the brain's decision. Then and only then his gun arm and hand would get the message and react."

"Is that how you've beaten so many opponents?" Doc asked. "By watching their eyes?"

"No," Clint said, "that only works when you're close to a man. When you're too far to see his eyes there's only one thing that keeps you alive."

"Being faster?"

Clint shook his head.

"Being more accurate. Getting your gun out fast doesn't help unless you can hit what you point at."

"He can hit what he aims at, all right."

"No, not what you *aim* at," Clint said, "I said what you *point* at. When you're in a situation where you have to produce your gun fast and fire it accurately, you have no time to aim. You have to be able to point a gun like it was your finger, and hit what you point at. Can he do that?"

Doc looked confused.

"I—I don't know. I never realized there was a difference between aiming and pointing."

"You don't have to know, Doc," Clint said. "You don't wear a gun."

"Thank God for that," Doc said. "Look, I'll let you rest. Will an hour be long enough?"

"That'll be fine."

Doc turned toward the door, then turned back.

"Founder's Day is only three days away."

"I know."

"If he is going to do something, he should do it before then, don't you agree?"

"Yes."

Doc hesitated, then said, "I hope you're ready."

"I hope so, too, Doc."

What none of the three men knew was that someone else was watching them, not only Mike Black. Mayor Ed Biggers heard that Clint Adams was out on the street and thought that the Kid would take the opportunity to make a name for himself. He watched from down the street, unable to hear what was being said, and was disappointed when the Kid sat back down and Doc and Clint went into the hotel.

"Don't be so disappointed."

Biggers turned and saw Mildred standing behind him. "What?"

"Don't be so disappointed," she repeated. "It'll probably happen soon."

Biggers scowled.

"What's the Kid waiting for?" he asked. "Adams is back on his feet."

"His feet and one crutch," Mildred said. "How would it look for the Kid to shoot down a man who was leaning on one crutch? No, he'll wait until Clint can stand without the crutch."

"Well, I hope he can throw that crutch away in the next couple of days," Biggers muttered.

"Why bother?" she asked. "Imagine what a story it would be if the Kid and Clint faced off right *on* Founder's Day. You wouldn't need fireworks."

Biggers thought a moment, then smiled and said, "You know, Mildred, you have a point."

FORTY-FOUR

Later that night Biggers walked into the saloon when he knew the poker game would be over and found the Kid sitting alone at a corner table.

"Mind if I sit, Kid?"

"You're the mayor, Mayor Ed," the Kid said.

Biggers took that as a yes and sat down.

"I have a proposition for you, Kid."

The younger man looked at him.

"Let's hear it."

Biggers leaned forward so no one else in the saloon would hear him, which was silly because there only three or four other men there, including the bartender.

"Five thousand dollars."

The Kid remained silent for a few moments, sipping his beer.

"For what?"

"For killing Clint Adams."

The Kid didn't respond.

"But you've got to do it on Founder's Day."

"That's the deal?" the Kid asked, after a few more moments.

"That's it, Kid. What do you think?"

157

"What do I think?" the Kid asked. Suddenly he tossed the rest of his beer into Biggers's face. The mayor sputtered and tried to wipe the beer off with his hands.

"What the—"

"I think you better get up and walk out of here right now, Mayor Ed, before I kill you . . . for free!"

"B-but w-why—w-what did I—"

"I'll kill Clint Adams when and where I please, and I'll do it for me. I've never killed anybody for money, and I don't intend to start now."

"I-I didn't mean—"

"Yes, you did," the Kid said. "Now get out—now!"

The other men in the saloon watched in surprise as Ed Biggers stood up, beer still dripping from him, turned and lurched through the batwing doors.

"Bartender," the Kid called out, "another beer."

Outside the saloon Biggers stopped and wiped the beer from his face with his sleeve. Who the hell did that little pip-squeak think he was? His fear from just moments ago was gone, replaced with a white-hot rage. Maybe he should go and make the same offer to Clint Adams now. He hoped Adams killed the Kid—but no. If anything, Adams would react even more violently to an offer of money for killing the Kid. Biggers was just going to have to watch and wait and see what happened, and if the Tucumcari Kid was the one who survived the encounter, he was going to have to figure out a way to pay him back for what he just did.

Biggers started for home, telling himself that he had at least saved himself five thousand dollars.

FORTY-FIVE

Clint woke the morning before Founder's Day with Mildred heavy on his left arm. He lay there for a few minutes, trying to figure out what was different, and then realized that his leg wasn't throbbing.

"What is it?" she asked, sensing something.

He smiled at her.

"My leg doesn't hurt."

"That's good," she said, rolling into him, putting her head on his shoulder. "That means tonight you can be on top."

"I'll have to check with my doctor on that."

She laughed, then ducked under the sheet. Moments later he was in her mouth, swelling and swelling as she sucked him, until he could swell no more without erupting. . . .

Later, while they were dressing, she suddenly stopped, sitting on the edge of the bed.

"What is it?"

"It's Biggers."

"The mayor? What about him?"

"He's setting you up."

159

"You mean with the Kid?"

She nodded.

"Is that what you've been wanting to tell me?"

She nodded again.

"And now you feel disloyal to him?"

Now she shook her head.

"Not anymore."

"Why not?"

"Because he's gone too far this time. He offered the Kid five thousand dollars to try to kill you."

"I think the Kid plans to do that for free."

"Ed wanted him to do it on Founder's Day."

"Well, that's tomorrow," Clint said. "Maybe that's what he's waiting for."

She turned to look at him.

"Either that, or for you to throw away that crutch."

"Could be."

"Do you hate me?"

He touched her face.

"Why? Because you felt loyalty to someone? No, I don't hate you."

"What are you going to do?"

"I've been thinking about that."

"And?"

"I'm going to talk to the Kid."

"About what?"

"I'm going to try to talk him out of this."

"Are you—do you think he might kill you?"

Clint laughed.

"Well, of course he might, but as it turns out, I like him. I'd hate to have to kill him. That's why I'm going to try to talk him out of it."

"Do you think you'll be able to?"

"I don't know," Clint said. "He's ruthless, and I think he likes it."

"Likes what?"

"The killing."

"Oh."

"But I'll give it a shot."

She made a face.

"That's a poor choice of words."

"Sorry."

She finished dressing and stood up. He was dressed except for his boots.

"I'm going to quit today."

"Not on my account, I hope."

"No," she said, "on mine."

"Good for you."

"When Founder's Day is over, I'm going to leave."

"And go where?"

"I don't think it matters."

He reached over and took her hand.

"I don't think it does either, Mildred," he said. "I think you'll make a good life for yourself wherever you go."

"I don't mind admitting I'm scared."

"That's okay," he said. "We're all scared."

"Even you?"

He nodded and said, "Yep, even me."

FORTY-SIX

When Avery came up with a pot of coffee at nine, Clint asked him to take a message to the Kid.

"Sure."

"Ask him to come here for coffee."

"That's it?"

"That's it."

"Just for coffee?"

Clint nodded and said, "Coffee."

"Okay," Avery said. "I'll tell him."

"Oh," Clint said, "and tell him not to bother to knock. I don't know if the door could stand up to it."

Since Avery usually brought two cups, Clint filled his own and set the other cup across the table from him, and waited.

The door opened fifteen minutes later and the Kid walked in.

"Mornin', Clint."

"Kid," Clint said. "We have to talk, and I thought we could do it over coffee."

"Sure thing."

The Kid sat and Clint poured him a cup. Utterly relaxed—or seemingly so—the Kid sat with his cup in his hand and asked, "What do we have to talk about?"

"You know that people are expecting us to try to kill one another."

"I know that."

"Especially Mayor Biggers."

The Kid chuckled.

"He's countin' on it."

"I understand he offered you some money to do it tomorrow."

"He did. I turned him down."

"Why?"

"I don't kill for money."

"Why kill at all?" Clint asked.

"I have my own reasons."

"You know," Clint said, "whichever one of us walks away will have helped Biggers achieve his goal."

"When I walk away," the Kid said, "I'll achieve my goal."

"Which is what?"

"Well, first, I'll have killed you and made a bigger reputation for myself."

"There's more?"

"Just a little," he said. "I told Mayor Ed I'd cut his little ribbon and oh, yeah, I get Mildred in my bed."

Clint narrowed his eyes.

"Has she agreed to this?"

"She does whatever Mayor Ed tells her."

"And do you?"

"No," the Kid said coldly.

"Then why do this?"

"I told you, I have my reasons. Is there some reason you don't want to do it?"

"I have no reason *to* do it, Kid."

"Sure, you do."

"Oh? And what's that?"

"You'll try to kill me because if you don't, I'll kill you."

Clint shook his head.

"This doesn't have to happen, Kid."

The Kid put his coffee down untouched and stood up.

"Yeah," he said, "it does."

Clint stared at the smaller, younger man for a few moments, then asked, "Is killing me going to make you taller, Harvey?"

He watched the Kid carefully, and was impressed. His face turned red at the use of his name, but he remained in control.

"A lot taller, Clint."

"I don't think so."

"Well, you don't have to," the Kid said. "All you have to know is that the minute, the second you toss that crutch away, I'm gonna kill you."

Clint said, "Kid—" But the young man was finished listening. He walked to the door and left the room without another word.

Clint shook his head and poured himself another cup of coffee. This was going to happen. It didn't seem that the Kid was going to give him much choice, but for it to happen tomorrow—for one of them to die on Founder's Day—would make Ed Biggers's day.

Clint had an idea. It was a dangerous one, depending on how good the Kid was with a gun, but there was only one way to find that out.

FORTY-SEVEN

When Doc Matthews arrived for the poker game Clint said, "Game's been canceled, Doc." He lifted his leg. "Get this thing off me."

While Doc removed the splint, Clint explained his plan to him.

"Do you think you can do that?"

"Who knows?" Clint said. "I've tried crazier things, though."

"If the Kid is as good with a gun as he says he is . . ." Doc said, leaving the rest unsaid.

"I know, Doc," Clint said, rubbing his leg now that the splint was off, "but I hate playing into Ed Biggers's hands."

"I don't blame you."

He told the doctor about Mildred's confession to him and her plans to leave town.

"Well," Doc said, "I guess I should make a confession, as well."

"About what, Doc? Don't tell me my leg wasn't really fractured?"

"Oh, it was fractured," Doc said, "but when I found

165

out who you were I went right to Ed Biggers with the information.''

''Why?''

''I knew he was looking for a celebrity.''

''No harm done, Doc.''

''No,'' Doc said, ''not until you go outside today.''

''Now,'' Clint said, ''I'm going out now.''

He put on his boots and then got up and walked gingerly around.

''Was the Kid sitting outside when you came in?''

''He was.''

''Might as well get this over with, then.'' He grabbed his crutch and shoved it under his arm. ''You going to come out and watch?''

''I might as well,'' Doc said. ''One of you is going to need me.''

The Kid was surprised when Clint came walking out of the hotel, followed by Doc.

''What's this?'' he asked. ''Bringing the game outside?''

''The game's over, Harvey,'' Clint said.

The Kid's face turned red again.

''Don't call me that.''

''Why not? It's your name, isn't it?''

''If you call me that,'' the Kid said, ''crutch or no crutch, I'll kill you.''

''Okay, then, Harvey,'' Clint said, ''let's try it with no crutch.''

Clint leaned the crutch against the hotel wall and left it there.

''You're ready for this?'' the Kid asked.

''I'm ready, Harvey.''

The Kid stood up quickly, and Clint thought he was going to charge him.

"You're tryin' to get me riled," the Kid said. "It ain't gonna work."

"Let's find out," Clint said, and he stepped into the street.

Mike Black, seeing what was going on, ran to tell Mayor Biggers. Both Biggers and Mildred came running in time to see it.

"Damn!" Biggers swore. "This wasn't supposed to happen until tomorrow."

"Enjoy it while you can, Ed."

"What the hell," Biggers said. "Today or tomorrow, as long as one of them dies."

"Listen to yourself," Mildred said. "You make me sick."

"What's the matter with you?" he demanded.

"You should know that after Founder's Day I'm leaving, Ed."

"Yeah?" He laughed. "Where will you go?"

"It doesn't matter," she said, "just as long as it's away from you. You've turned into someone I don't want to know."

"We'll talk about this later . . ." he said, and directed his attention to the two men in the street.

Clint walked out to the center of the street, still taking most of his weight on his uninjured leg. He was making every effort, though, to show no ill effects.

He watched carefully as the Kid walked into the center of the street, as well. He knew what he was going to try to do was dangerous, but it was all he could think of.

''This is it, Clint,'' the Kid said.

''Go ahead, Harvey,'' Clint said. ''Throw your life away.''

There were more people on the street than Clint had seen since arriving in Tucumcari.

''Son of a bitch—'' Harvey Little, alias the Tucumcari Kid, said, and went for his gun.

The Kid was good. Clint could see that as soon as his hand started moving. He even cleared leather by the time Clint fired, but he didn't have time to bring the gun up. Clint fired once and the bullet struck the Kid just below his left knee. He cried out and fell to the ground. If Clint had put the bullet right in his knee he would have crippled the Kid for life, but that wasn't his intention. His intention was for neither of them to die, thereby ruining Ed Biggers's plan. In the past he'd never shot to wound, because it was too risky, but he thought the risk was worth it this time.

When Clint drew, it was the fastest thing Doc, Mike Black, Mildred, Mayor Biggers, or any of the others had ever seen in their lives.

''God!'' Biggers said. But in the next moment, when he realized what was happening, that his plans for Founder's Day and for Tucumcari were ruined, he added, ''Damn!''

Mildred clapped her hands together and said under her breath to Clint, ''Good for you.''

Doc heaved a sigh of relief, gratified that Clint's plan had worked, but knowing that he now had himself another patient, one who would be around a lot longer than Clint.

The pain in the Kid's leg was unbearable. His brain was telling him to fire his gun, but his body was not responding. His hand opened, releasing his gun, and with both hands he reached for his wounded leg.

The Kid was rolling on the ground, holding his knee, his gun lying forgotten in the dirt. Clint looked around, spotted Ed Biggers, and glared at him for a moment. He could see the disappointment on the man's face. He was going to have to wait a little longer to get his town on the map. This little incident wouldn't do it.

Clint holstered his gun, walked over to where he'd left the crutch, picked it up and walked over to the Kid, who stared up at him.

"My leg—" he said.

"Here," Clint said, dropping the crutch next to him, "you need this more than I do."

SPECIAL PREVIEW

They were the most brutal gang of cutthroats ever assembled. And during the Civil War, they sought justice outside of the law. Paying back every Yankee raid with one of their own. They rode hard, shot straight, and had their way with every willing woman west of the Mississippi. No man could stop them. No woman could resist them. And no Yankee stood a chance of living when Quantrill's Raiders rode into town . . .

BUSHWHACKERS
by B. J. Lanagan

Available in paperback from Jove Books

And now here's a special excerpt from
this thrilling new series . . .

Jackson County, Missouri, 1862

As Seth Coulter lay his pocket watch on the bedside table and blew out the lantern, he thought he saw a light outside. Walking over to the window, he pulled the curtain aside to stare out into the darkness.

On the bed alongside him the mattress creaked, and his wife, Irma, raised herself on her elbows.

"What is it, Seth?" Irma asked. "What are you lookin' at?"

"Nothin', I reckon."

"Well, you're lookin' at somethin'."

"Thought I seen a light out there, is all."

Seth continued to look through the window for a moment longer. He saw only the moon-silvered West Missouri hills.

"A light? What on earth could that be at this time of night?" Irma asked.

"Ah, don't worry about it," Seth replied, still looking through the window. "It's prob'ly just lightning bugs."

"Lightning bugs? Never heard of lightning bugs this early in the year."

"Well it's been a warm spring," Seth explained. Finally, he came away from the window, projecting to his wife an easiness he didn't feel. "I'm sure it's nothing," he said.

"I reckon you're right," the woman agreed. "Wisht the boys was here, though."

Seth climbed into bed. He thought of the shotgun over

the fireplace mantel in the living room, and he wondered if he should go get it. He considered it for a moment, then decided against it. It would only cause Irma to ask questions, and just because he was feeling uneasy, was no reason to cause her any worry. He turned to her and smiled.

"What do you want the boys here for?" he asked. "If the boys was here, we couldn't be doin' this." Gently, he began pulling at her nightgown.

"Seth, you old fool, what do you think you're doin'?" Irma scolded. But there was a lilt of laughter in her voice, and it was husky, evidence that far from being put off by him, she welcomed his advances.

Now, any uneasiness Seth may have felt fell away as he tugged at her nightgown. Finally she sighed.

"You better let me do it," she said. "Clumsy as you are, you'll like-as-not tear it."

Irma pulled the nightgown over her head, then dropped it onto the floor beside her bed. She was forty-six years old, but a lifetime of hard work had kept her body trim, and she was proud of the fact that she was as firm now as she had been when she was twenty. She lay back on the bed and smiled up at her husband, her skin glowing silver in the splash of moonlight. Seth ran his hand down her nakedness, and she trembled under his touch. He marvelled that, after so many years of marriage, she could still be so easily aroused.

Three hundred yards away from the house Emil Slaughter, leader of a band of Jayhawkers, twisted around in his saddle to look back at the dozen or so riders with him. Their faces were fired orange in the flickering lights of the torches. Felt hats were pulled low, and they were all wearing long dusters, hanging open to provide access to the pistols which protruded from their belts. His band of followers looked, Slaughter thought, as if a fissure in the earth had suddenly opened to allow a legion of demons to escape from hell. There was about them a hint of sulphur.

A hint of sulphur. Slaughter smiled at the thought. He liked that idea. Such an illusion would strike fear into the hearts of his victims, and the more frightened they were, the easier it would be for him to do his job.

Quickly, Slaughter began assigning tasks to his men.

"You two hit the smokehouse, take ever' bit of meat they got a'curin'."

"Hope they got a couple slabs of bacon," someone said.

"I'd like a ham or two," another put in.

"You three, go into the house. Clean out the pantry, flour, corn-meal, sugar, anything they got in there. And if you see anything valuable in the house, take it too."

"What about the people inside?"

"Kill 'em," Slaughter said succinctly.

"Women, too?"

"Kill 'em all."

"What about their livestock?"

"If they got 'ny ridin' horses, we'll take 'em. The plowin' animals, we'll let burn when we torch the barn. All right, let's go."

In the bedroom Seth and Irma were oblivious to what was going on outside. Seth was over her, driving himself into her moist triangle. Irma's breathing was coming faster and more shallow as Seth gripped her buttocks with his hands, pulling her up to meet him. He could feel her fingers digging into his shoulders, and see her jiggling, sweat-pearled breasts as her head flopped from side to side with the pleasure she was feeling.

Suddenly Seth was aware of a wavering, golden glow on the walls of the bedroom. A bright light was coming through the window.

"What the hell?" he asked, interrupting the rhythm and, holding himself up from her on stiffened arms, one hand on each side of her head.

"No, no," Irma said through clenched teeth. "Don't stop now, don't . . ."

"Irma, my God! The barn's on fire!" Seth shouted, as he disengaged himself.

"What?" Irma asked, now also aware of the orange glow in the room.

Seth got out of bed and started quickly to pull on his trousers. Suddenly there was a crashing sound from the front of the house as the door was smashed open.

"Seth!" Irma screamed.

Drawing up his trousers, Seth started toward the living room and the shotgun he had over the fireplace.

"You lookin' for this, you Missouri bastard?" someone asked. He was holding Seth's shotgun.

"Who the hell are . . ." That was as far as Seth got. His question was cut off by the roar of the shotgun as a charge of double-aught buckshot slammed him back against the wall. He slid down to the floor, staining the wall behind him with blood and guts from the gaping exit wounds in his back.

"Seth! My God, no!" Irma shouted, running into the living room when she heard the shotgun blast. So concerned was she about her husband that she didn't bother to put on her nightgown.

"Well, now, lookie what we got here," a beady-eyed Jayhawker said, staring at Irma's nakedness. "Boys, I'm goin' to have me some fun."

"No," Irma said, shaking now, not only in fear for her own life, but in shock from seeing her husband's lifeless body leaning against the wall.

Beady Eyes reached for Irma.

"Please," Irma whimpered. She twisted away from him. "Please."

"Listen to her beggin' me for it, boys. Lookit them titties! Damn, she's not a bad-lookin' woman, you know that?" His dark beady eyes glistened, rat-like, as he opened his pants then reached down to grab himself. His erection projected forward like a club.

"No, please, don't do this," Irma pleaded.

"You wait 'til I stick this cock in you, honey," Beady Eyes said. "Hell, you goin' to like it so much you'll think you ain't never been screwed before."

Irma turned and ran into the bedroom. The others followed her, laughing, until she was forced against the bed.

"Lookit this, boys! She's brought me right to her bed! You think this bitch ain't a'wantin' it?"

"I beg of you, if you've any kindness in you . . . Irma started, but her plea was interrupted when Beady Eyes backhanded her so savagely that she fell across the bed, her mouth filled with blood.

"Shut up!" he said, harshly. "I don't like my women talkin' while I'm diddlin' 'em!"

Beady Eyes came down onto the bed on top of her, then he spread her legs and forced himself roughly into her. Irma felt as if she were taking a hot poker inside her, and she cried out in pain.

"Listen to her squealin'. He's really givin' it to her," one of the observers said.

Beady Eyes wheezed and gasped as he thrust into her roughly.

"Don't wear it out none," one of the others giggled. "We'uns want our turn!"

At the beginning of his orgasm, Beady Eyes enhanced his pleasure by one extra move that was unobserved by the others. Immediately thereafter he felt the convulsive tremors of the woman beneath him, and that was all it took to trigger his final release. He surrendered himself to the sensation of fluid and energy rushing out of his body, while he groaned and twitched in orgiastic gratification.

"Look at that! He's comin' in the bitch right now!" one of the others said excitedly. "Damn! You wait 'til I get in there! I'm goin' to come in quarts!"

Beady Eyes lay still on top of her until he had spent his final twitch, then he got up. She was bleeding from a stab wound just below her left breast.

"My turn," one of the others said, already taking out his cock. He had just started toward her when he saw the wound in the woman's chest, and the flat look of her dead eyes. "What the hell?" he asked. "What happened to her?"

The second man looked over at Beady Eyes in confusion. Then he saw Beady Eyes wiping blood off the blade of his knife.

"You son of bitch!" he screamed in anger. "You kilt her!"

"Slaughter told us to kill her," Beady Eyes replied easily.

"Well, you could'a waited 'til someone else got a

chance to do her before you did it, you bastard!'' The second man, putting himself back into his pants, started toward Beady Eyes when, suddenly, there was the thunder of a loud pistol shot.

''What the hell is going on in here?'' Slaughter yelled. He was standing just inside the bedroom door, holding a smoking pistol in his hand, glaring angrily at them.

''This son of a bitch kilt the woman while he was doin' her!''

''We didn't come here to screw,'' Slaughter growled. ''We come here to get supplies.''

''But he kilt her *while* he was screwin' her! Who would do somethin' like that?''

''Before, during, after, what difference does it make?'' Slaughter asked. ''As long as she's dead. Now, you've got work to do, so get out there in the pantry, like I told you, and start gatherin' up what you can. You,'' he said to Beady Eyes, ''go through the house, take anything you think we can sell. I want to be out of here in no more'n five minutes.''

''Emil, what woulda been the harm in us havin' our turn?''

Slaughter cocked the pistol and pointed it at the one who was still complaining. ''The harm is, I told you not to,'' he said. ''Now, do you want to debate the issue?''

''No, no!'' the man said quickly, holding his hands out toward Slaughter. ''Didn't mean nothin' by it. I was just talkin', that's all.''

''Good,'' Slaughter said. He looked over at Beady Eyes. ''And you. If you ever pull your cock out again without me sayin' it's all right, I'll cut the goddamned thing off.''

''It wasn't like you think, Emil,'' Beady Eyes said.

"I was just tryin' to be easy on the woman, is all. I figured it would be better if she didn't know it was about to happen."

Slaughter shook his head. "You're one strange son of a bitch, you know that?" He stared at the three men for a minute, then he shook his head in disgust as he put his pistol back into his belt. "Get to work."

Beady Eyes was the last one out and as he started to leave he saw, lying on the chifforobe, a gold pocket watch. He glanced around to make sure no one was looking. Quickly, and unobserved, he slipped the gold watch into his own pocket.

This was a direct violation of Slaughter's standing orders. Anything of value found on any of their raids was to be divided equally among the whole. That meant that, by rights, he should give the watch to Slaughter, who would then sell it and divide whatever money it brought. But because it was loot, they would be limited as to where they could sell the watch. That meant it would bring much less than it was worth and by the time it was split up into twelve parts, each individual part would be minuscule. Better, by far, that he keep the watch for himself.

Feeling the weight of the watch riding comfortably in his pocket, he went into the pantry to start clearing it out.

"Lookie here!" the other man detailed for the pantry said. "This here family ate pretty damn good, I'll tell you. We've made us quite a haul: flour, coffee, sugar, onions, potatoes, beans, peas, dried peppers."

"Yeah, if they's as lucky in the smokehouse, we're goin' to feast tonight!"

The one gathering the loot came into the pantry then,

holding a bulging sack. "I found some nice gold candlesticks here, too," he said. "We ought to get somethin' for them."

"You men inside! Let's go!" Slaughter's shout came to them.

The Jayhawkers in the house ran outside where Slaughter had brought everyone together. Here, they were illuminated by the flames of the already-burning barn. Two among the bunch were holding flaming torches, and they looked at Slaughter expectantly.

With a nod of his head, Slaughter said, "All right, burn the rest of the buildings now."

Watch for

THE ORIENT EXPRESS

188th novel in the exciting GUNSMITH series
from Jove

Coming in August!

J. R. ROBERTS
THE
GUNSMITH